HELP*!* I Gotta Sell My Car NOW*!*
NEW RULES for Selling Your Vehicle Online

By L. James Johnson

Edited by David Carr

A Lone Wolf Consortium Book

Published by
Lone Wolf Consortium
El Cerrito, CA
www.LoneWolfConsortium.com

Editor: David Carr – www.MovingWords.us
Marketing Consultant: Tomar Levine – www.YourTimeToBloom.com
Book Design: Pat Power – www.PatPowerDesign.com

For information, consulting, live events, speaker bookings—or interviews for radio, TV, print, or online sources—and other services, please visit the **Media** page at www.BayAreaCarGuy.com/media or email james@BayAreaCarGuy.com.

ISBN 978-1-935736-00-4

Library of Congress Control Number: 2010910057

Printed in the United States of America.

Dedication

This book is dedicated to Rob Wilbur. Rob took me under his wing and taught me about the car business, people, and life. It was through Rob I learned firsthand that surviving the shark tank of a dealership is not enough. It is possible to have integrity in delicately balancing the best interests of my customers, the dealership, and myself.

Special thanks to:

David Carr – Editor. As an editor, David is stalwart in his ability to hold the voice and the vision of the project through to the end. His capacity for clarifying my thoughts—along with my writing—is uncanny. And his brilliance in discovering that rare gem in a random pile of manuscripts was instrumental in making *HELP! I Gotta Sell My Car NOW!* possible. www.MovingWords.us

Tomar Levine – Marketing Consultant. Tomar is a kindred spirit whose entrepreneurial fearlessness cannot be denied. This twin path we have explored over the last 16 years now includes following this intricate thread through the worlds of writing, communication, marketing, web design, publishing, and so much more. www.YourTimeToBloom.com

The Lone Wolf Consortium. David, Tomar and myself are the charter members of the Lone Wolf Consortium, an entrepreneurial gathering place for those of us interested in the Internet, marketing, and publishing. There is strength in numbers, even for lone wolves. This is a Lone Wolf Consortium book. www.LoneWolfConsortium.com

Get Online Resources for Selling Your Car
at www.BayAreaCarGuy.com

BayAreaCarGuy.com is a companion website to *HELP! I Gotta Sell My Car NOW!* Discover these resources:

- **Photo page** – Photo layouts for all major websites. Discover which photos to use and the order to upload when posting your ad online.

- **Video page** – Examples of how to record your video walk-around. This is the secret weapon that's easy to use. Become a YouTube star.

- **Tools page** – Tons of other FREE tools to help you sell your car.

- **Need Help? page** – Two services offered depending on your level of expertise:

  - **The Quick Consult** – One for private sellers and one for car dealers. I'm available to answer questions, including—for private sellers—how to price your car.

  - **Write My Ad** – The name says it all. Private sellers get an effective ad and a pricing strategy. I also check in weekly until your car sells. It's like having your personal Automotive Consultant on call.

Also written by L. James Johnson

The 8 Biggest Mistakes Used Car Buyers Make And How to Avoid Them!

DOWNLOAD
FREE PDF

PDF (3.15mb)
Adobe

Download your FREE 18-page PDF online at www.BayAreaCarGuy.com

Here is what auto professionals have to say about *The 8 Biggest Mistakes*:

"Don't buy a used car without reading The 8 Biggest Mistakes."
Stephanie Peters
Internet Sales Manager & 15-year car industry veteran

"A quick read. 18 pages that can save you thousands of dollars."
Rob Wilbur
Used Car Manager & 25-year car industry veteran

Table of Contents

1 NEW RULES for Selling Vehicles Online

Even the Pros are Having A Hard Time Figuring It Out

You, my reader, owe thanks to my friend Fred for calling me to unload his troubles. He lost his job and was only halfway through paying off the loan on his gas-guzzling 2006 Cadillac Escalade. With a wife and two kids to feed, *he was in big trouble.*

Before he called, Fred spent months trying to sell his SUV online. He posted pictures and a description of the vehicle on free websites like Craigslist. He also paid hundreds of dollars on "premium" used car sites. Nothing came of it except a single inquiry that didn't pan out. Was it bad timing, Fred?

Meanwhile, he was making monthly payments out of his dwindling savings on his keep-up-with-the-neighbors Escalade that burned so much gas he could barely afford to back it out of the garage.

Fred finally called me for help. He knew I had recently left my job as Internet Sales Manager for an auto dealership. I had been responsible for online marketing of used cars, trucks and SUVs.

*I was the professional who survived
by selling millions of dollars of used cars
on the very websites that had failed him.*

It was a smart move on his part.

So How Do You Go About It?

You've been scratching your head wondering how to word your ad, what pictures to show, what details to include, and—probably the biggest challenge—what price to ask.

I'm here to tell you that selling used cars online is difficult for dealers as well as folks like you. However, it's a process no one can ignore because it's becoming the prime place for marketing pre-owned vehicles.

It wasn't long ago...

We can count in months, not years, that car dealers began scrambling because used car buyers were checking out what was online before wandering onto the dealer's lot.

It's no longer strangers slinking in and saying,
"Help! I need a used car."

Today, most used car buyers have been online before they ever walk into a dealership. And dealers have been forced to adapt (some kicking and screaming)—by building an Internet sales department, re-directing advertising budgets, and re-considering how they price their vehicles.

*Don't tell them I said so, but many large auto dealers
do a poor job of marketing their vehicles online.*

They know a lot about print advertising, but fewer buyers are looking in newspapers or auto/shopper magazines—and why bother? They're out of date by the time they're delivered. The cars pictured may have been sold before the paper went to press!

Many "old school" car dealers simply haven't figured out the New Rules for effectively marketing their vehicles online. Unfortunately for them, they won't get a second chance to create a first impression.

You Can Learn, Too!

If professionals are having a difficult time staying ahead of the learning curve, you shouldn't feel bad if you are not clear on how to effectively sell your car, truck, or SUV on the Internet.

It's barely three years since I was asked to decipher the mysteries of online marketing, and to design the best method for selling used (my boss insisted on "pre-owned") vehicles on sites like AutoTrader, Cars.com, Craigslist, and Kijiji. Luckily, I worked for a forward-thinking company that trusted me to experiment, knowing I'd make mistakes that we could learn from. How else to learn?

It took a year of trial and error to develop a clean, effective format for our online postings and ads. But that was only part of the learning curve.

I discovered that there is a weekly shopping cycle
specific to online buyers. Unless you time your ads correctly,
much of your effort could be wasted.

We also learned how important pictures and pricing are to attract potential buyers and complete the sale.

Developing **New Rules** for marketing used vehicles online was intense work. But our sales volume increased, and we drew buyers from farther and farther away.

Customers regularly drove two, three, and, in one case, five and a half hours one-way just to check out a car we'd posted. And virtually every customer who drove that distance bought the vehicle they came to see.

Think about it. What would entice someone to drive eleven hours round trip to look at a used car?

5 NEW RULES for Selling Vehicles Online

1. Bold Headline
2. Detailed Information
3. Personal Touches
4. Specific Photos
5. Video Walk-Around

The New Rules

Bold Headline
First, the subject line has to grab attention away from all the competing ads—and for some models there may be hundreds posted.

Detailed Information
The text must be clear and concise, specifying all the information a buyer cares about in order to determine if *your* vehicle is worth the time to look at.

Personal Touches
Personal touches will sweeten your posting—information that only someone who cared about the vehicle would know. These make the seller seem trustworthy. Emphasize the positive AND tell the truth about the condition of the vehicle.

Specific Photos
Seeing the features and accessories that *your* buyer is looking for will catch her attention.

Video Walk-Around

Finally, the secret weapon that induces someone to drive eleven hours is the video walk-around. It's a simple tool I love to use, even if my customer is in the neighborhood, and it's easy to put together.

It builds an enormous amount of trust and rapport between buyer and seller, providing a load of information quickly. I know the video walk-around sealed the deal for my buyers even before they came over to see the car. There's a step-by-step guide to creating your own walk-around in Chapter 10.

A Happy Ending

Even though the market was down and few people were interested in a luxury, gas-guzzling SUV like Fred's Escalade, he sold it just *six days* after we posted the first *free* online ad.

We didn't venture onto premium websites that charge a fee. And Fred was thrilled to sell his Escalade for *more* than the bank loan, which put much needed cash in his pocket.

Thanks to Fred's troubles, I've put what I learned from a year of trial and error into *HELP! I Gotta Sell My Car NOW!* so you'll benefit from my insider knowledge of the auto industry.

This is your best tool for *profitably* selling your used vehicle *quickly*, even in a competitive market and difficult financial times.

> *The purpose of this book is to*
> *help you learn from the professionals,*
> *and to sell your vehicle*
> *for its full market value—quickly!*

Good luck, and for goodness' sake try to *have fun* with the process.

2 Getting Your Vehicle Ready

Common Sense Suggestions that will Put Money in Your Pocket

Major auto dealers sell millions of dollars of used cars every month. They make their vehicles as clean, tidy, polished, and attractive as possible. Some call it "curb appeal." It works!

Whether you are selling a luxury sedan or an old clunker: a clean and spiffed-up vehicle will sell quicker and for more money than one with halitosis—unwashed, grimy, and strewn with unwanted papers and moldy fast food containers.

You want to seduce your potential buyer,
not turn them off with a bad first impression.
It's worth the time and effort to do it right.

Be appropriate for the value and condition of your vehicle. For example, a quick wash and vacuum is probably all that is needed for a $1200 Ford Taurus.

However, if you are selling an $8,000 Toyota Camry, you probably want to invest in a wax job and deeper cleaning from grille to trunk. For a Lexus or Escalade, even more tasteful care is needed.

No matter what you want to sell, check the list below and do what is appropriate for *your* vehicle. Fronting the cash to have it detailed by a professional may pay for itself—and even put money in your pocket.

Basic services run from $15 to $50, and $100 to $300 for a full-service, professional detail job that will leave it sparkling inside and out. Don't be shy with a professional detailer: request a price quote. Then call around for the best deal—with them, *you* are a buyer.

Exterior

- **Wash**
- **Wax**

- **Cut polish**

  Use a "cut polish" (also known as "cut wax") to remove light scratches or scrapes on the paint. This can bring a degraded, flat finish back to life.

  Vehicles are manufactured with many layers of paint. Cut polish contains a mild abrasive that removes the first layer or so, revealing a fresh finish that hasn't been dulled by oxidation. Small scrapes or scratches virtually disappear. Larger ones can be reduced in size. The investment can add hundreds of dollars to your sale.

- **Alloy rims**

  If your vehicle has premium or after market rims, spend a few minutes cleaning each one. Special cleansers are available from auto parts stores.

  This is where you need to decide what is appropriate: if special tires and rims are a major selling point, it's worth the investment. Use a tire gloss to help them look their best.

- **Engine**

  If the engine is dirty, oily and grimy, it needs washing. Because of all the electrical wires and hoses that can be damaged, I won't wash the engine on my own car.

  If you have doubts about doing it yourself, let a professional auto detailer boost your sale for you. (They also need work these days.)

Interior

- Remove all personal items from the interior, trunk, and glove box.

- Vacuum the seats and under the seats, the carpet and the floor mats. Don't forget to take the floor mats out and vacuum under them.

- Wipe down all interior surfaces. Use a vinyl protector like *Armor All* on the dash and other surfaces to give a clean shine. Don't forget the doors, arm rests, steering wheel and column, and all those cubby holes and storage places that collect clutter and dust.

- Wash the windows with a glass cleaner—inside and out—along with the mirrors (interior and exterior).

Miscellaneous

- Top off all fluid levels—engine oil, windshield washer fluid, power steering fluid, and coolant.

- Inflate tires to the correct pressure.

- Tip – A quick lube facility will change the engine oil, top off all fluids, and make sure the tires are at the correct pressure, quickly and inexpensively.

- Replace burned out fuses and lights. A quick lube facility may do this as well.

- Some buyers will want to have the vehicle inspected by their own mechanic. But it may be worthwhile to have *your* mechanic perform a pre-purchase inspection. Have that report available for an interested buyer. Cost? Under $200. It's another confidence builder.

- Not sure which local companies to deal with? Would you prefer to work with a national company that provides standardized third-party pre-purchase inspections? I can help with both. Look on my **Tools** page at www.BayAreaCarGuy.com/tools.

Gather Records

- **Vehicle history report**
  Build trust and credibility with a prospective purchaser by offering them as much information about your car as possible. Unless your car has been in an accident or has other issues, a vehicle history report is a good place to start.

  Most people are familiar with the brand names Carfax and Auto-Check, the two largest suppliers of vehicle history. These reports have become indispensable for used car buyers. A vehicle history report tells the buyer:

  — if the car was ever in an accident or had a salvage title[1]

  — if it was damaged by Katrina, Ike, or another natural disaster

  — if it was a lemon buyback

---

[1] If a vehicle is classified as a total loss following a serious accident, it is issued a special "salvage" title by the DMV prior to resale.

— if its mileage was falsified by rolling back the odometer

— how many owners it has had (a one-owner vehicle generally has higher resale value)

— in which city and state the vehicle has been registered, serviced, and sold

Which vehicle history report should you use? Save up to 40% by making the right choice. See my recommendation, including a cost comparison, at www.BayAreaCarGuy.com/historyreports.

- **Service records**

  Especially for major work recently completed. This will help build confidence in the reliability of the vehicle, and it's proof that you have kept it well maintained.

- Your mechanic's pre-purchase inspection report, if available.

- Current vehicle registration.

- Current vehicle insurance.

- Title.

- Don't have a title, even though your car is paid off, because the lending institution went belly up? Contact the Federal Deposit Insurance Corporation at 1-888-206-4662.

- No title because you still have a bank loan?

  – Gather loan documents.

  – **10-day payoff figure**
    Call your lender and ask for the "10-day payoff" figure (that's how much you will owe them if you pay the balance of your loan within the next ten days). Make note of the amount, and also have them email or fax you a copy.

Ask yourself what investment of time, energy, and money will put the most cash in your pocket and create the easiest sale?

Then step into your buyer's shoes by asking yourself:

- What would put *me* at ease if I were the one out shopping for a used vehicle?

- How would I want the car presented so I could evaluate the features that matter the most?

After that it's simple!

Do what you think will work—and what you can afford.

3 | Pricing Your Vehicle

Learning from the Professionals

Establishing the price of a vehicle is a make or break issue for both dealers and private sellers. Unfortunately, pricing used vehicles is not an exact science. In fact, it usually comes down to making your "best guess," then testing that price in the marketplace to see if it's realistic.

Each pre-owned vehicle is one-of-a-kind. No other vehicle in the world is just like yours, with the exact mileage or in the same condition. Yours is unique, and therefore its market price is too. However, **until you have a willing buyer, the market value is unknown.** That is why car dealers use a pricing strategy that balances:

- their chances of selling a car quickly, with
- maximizing the amount of money they will make on the sale

Don't quit here: I'll reveal details of the dealers' method shortly.

Lots of Variables

Because of the wild west nature of selling used cars, dealers regularly make mistakes that cost them money, even a lot of money. There are simply too many variables that affect the selling price of a used car:

- the time of year
- the price of gas
- the economy
- interest rates
- availability of financing
- the supply of used cars
- the demand for used cars
- wholesale prices
- the neighborhood/locale ("local conditions")

And the totally unpredictable, including government programs like Cash for Clunkers. Demand for a specific make or model can be hot one week and frigid the next. In this constantly changing environment, dealers and private sellers need a healthy dose of intuition and experience—along with market research—to calculate their "best guess" as they formulate a pricing strategy versus a single price that remains current until the vehicle is sold.[2]

Barriers You Erect that Block the Sale

Before setting the initial price, let's look at other issues besides fair market value. Like personal ones. Overpricing gets more people in trouble than any other aspect of the selling process. Why is this important? Most buyers are already online comparing your price against other postings. If you set a price that is too high, no one will even bother clicking on your listing.

Sellers price themselves out of the market for a variety of reasons, including:

- being emotionally attached to their vehicle

- believing that their vehicle is still worth what they paid for it, or (worse) what they owe on it

- believing they should be able to recoup the cost of accessories, like a spoiler and roof rack, as well as after-market items like a GPS device, alarm system and premium wheels

- believing they should recoup tax and license fees

- not understanding that a dealer can almost always get a better price than a private seller

- not reducing the price in spite of needed repairs or less-than-ideal condition, given its year and mileage

Insider Information

"Fair market value" is whatever a willing buyer will pay a willing seller.

In practical terms, this means that a vehicle is worth what someone will pay for it ***now***!

---

[2] Progressive dealers are using new software tools that take a significant amount of the guessing out of pricing pre-owned vehicles. Programs such as FirstLook and vAuto let a dealer know exactly where their vehicle is priced compared to all other dealer vehicles for sale online that day.

The truth is: the price you get for your vehicle has nothing to do with what you still owe, the add-ons or accessories that came with the car (unless they have value for the buyer), or the fact that you're sentimental about it because it was Aunt Bessie's car before she developed Alzheimer's.

Instead, the balance you are looking for is:

- to sell your vehicle *fast,* and to get every penny the buyer is willing to part with ("not leaving money on the table" is how the pros talk about it).

What Dealers Face

Dealers who have huge inventories of pre-owned vehicles primarily consider two things as they develop a pricing strategy:

- By setting the **Initial Selling Price** on the high end of the price range, they are increasing their chance of making a bigger profit.

- If the dealer can't "max out," they *slowly* lower the price. When it sells they know what the market will bear.

Even though dealers *want* to sell their vehicles quickly—certainly in the first 30 days—most dealers *need* to sell them within two to three months.

Dealers (or their banks) have laid out real cash to build up inventory. If a car sits around hogging precious space, their investment turns into an expense, rather than a profit-generator.

With that reality in mind, their pricing strategy determines how quickly the price is dropped, and by how much it is lowered in each step.

If a dealer drops a price too quickly, they may be leaving money on the table— shamed before their boss by the ultimate sin of the industry. If they're too greedy and keep the price high for too long, the vehicle is unlikely to sell.

They need to keep their money working, not letting it lounge about in a pretty showroom. If a dealer follows the training manual and gradually lowers the price, chances are a customer will buy somewhere in the range that nets the business a reasonable return.

If done wrong, there will come a moment
when they must drastically slash the price—
taking a loss just to get it off their lot and
put their capital back in action.

So a smart shopper can wrangle a very good deal by knowing exactly how to use the dealer's system against them. Stay tuned—that's my next book.

Fair Market Value

In fact, a vehicle's "fair market value" *is* what
a buyer is willing to pay for it right now—today—this very moment.

To Sum Up

Here's what we're keeping in mind:

Goals

1. Selling within a short time frame.

2. Maximizing income.

Market Reality

1. No other vehicle is exactly like yours.

2. There's competition from other sellers.

Strategy

1. Determine an acceptable price range.

2. Best guess: List at the highest selling price you are comfortable with.

3. Lower it slowly—there might not be a buyer today, but there could be one in three days.

Now Let's Get to Work:
The Nuts and Bolts of Used Car Pricing

Establish the Price Range

Kelley Blue Book is the source of your figures. FREE. You'll find what you need at www.kbb.com. The site is simple to use. It will lead you through a series of options, starting with *New* or *Used*. All you do is click the listed option that applies in each window.

KBB will give you the *Retail Value* and the *Private Party Value* for your vehicle.

- **The KBB "Suggested Retail Value"** is an average dealer's **Initial Selling Price** for a vehicle like yours, not the *expected* selling price. Dealers start high so they have wiggle room, knowing that they will probably negotiate a lower price in order to move the vehicle off the lot and into the bank.

- **The KBB "Private Party Value"** is what a buyer can expect to pay for *your* vehicle. In other words, this is what the car is likely to sell for when *you* sell it.

Insert figures for your car in this chart. This is the price range that your vehicle *could* sell for:

Used Car Price Range

KBB Suggested Retail Value $_____

KBB Private Party Value $_____

Determine Your Initial Selling Price

This is the first and highest price to post. **Only *you* can determine this figure**. It should fall between KBB's Suggested Retail Value and the Private Party Value.

In simple terms, if the Private Party Value is your expected selling price, you want to add your own wiggle room on top of that. Most prospective buyers will make you an offer that is lower than that no matter how low you set the Initial Selling Price. Also, the Private Party Value is Kelley's best guess, based on recent sales. It may not be accurate for your *unique* vehicle, in your market *today*.

Factors to consider in setting the Initial Selling Price:

- **Condition** – Be honest in selecting KBB's category that most accurately describes your vehicle's condition: Excellent, good, or fair. Only 1 in 20 used vehicles are actually in excellent condition. Most are Good.

  Read the descriptions and choose accordingly. (If you think yours falls under Poor, read what KBB says about pricing it.)

- **Time** – How quickly do you need to sell your vehicle? The quicker you need to sell it, the lower the price should be.

- **Money** – How much do you need to recoup from the sale? If you have a loan on the vehicle, or if you need to maximize your profit, choose the higher end of the price range. But be prepared to wait longer for a buyer and recognize that needing to maximize your profit doesn't mean that the market with oblige with a higher price.

- **Uniqueness** – Was your convertible used to drive Lana Turner to the Homecoming Game at Central High in 1938? Maybe it has a custom after-market metallic paint job with "bling" wheels.

  Your vehicle's uniqueness certainly has meaning to you. The secret is finding a buyer who also appreciates its rarity or peculiarity *and is willing to pay extra for those features*. In general, a car priced for unique features will take longer to sell than a standard car because there are fewer buyers who care.

Double Check Your Price

Use common sense to confirm your Initial Selling Price. Here are some websites to check for a sense of what similar vehicles are going for in your area. Adjust your price based on what you discover:

- Edmunds.com. They publish a True Market Value (TMV) for pre-owned vehicles, similar to KBB's Private Party Value. It's a good comparison tool. In fact, if Edmunds' figures for Private Party or Retail are higher than KBB's numbers, go ahead and use them. If your buyer balks, tell them where you found the info. Don't forget—buyers use the Internet, too.

- Craigslist.org

- Kijiji.com

- Backpage.com

- AutoTrader.com

- Cars.com

Be sure to compare apples to apples, meaning look at vehicles that are the same year, make, model, trim level, transmission (automatic or manual), engine size, mileage, accessories, and condition as yours. Because of uniqueness, this not always possible, so trust your judgment.

If your price is too high, you'll know by how slowly your vehicle sells. If you are flooded with calls the first day, it's probably priced too low and you're leaving money on the table. Adjust the Initial Selling Price based on your results.

Be Realistic

You're not a dealer. Dealers virtually always
sell a vehicle for more than a private seller can.
(If not, they won't be in business very long.)
Consider Retail Value as a dealer price,
and put more weight on private sellers' prices.

Variable Price Factors

The used car market has become more volatile over the last few years. This means that prices can change quickly and vary region to region and model to model. Use common sense. Here are some factors to take into account:

- **Gas prices** – Price at the pump creates more volatility in the market than anything else. When gas prices are high, larger vehicles including SUVs plummet in value. This also inflates the value of smaller fuel-efficient vehicles, especially hybrids, sub-compacts and small SUVs. The reverse tends to happen when gas prices fall.

- **Seasonal changes** – 4-wheel drives are in greater demand going into fall and winter. Demand decreases come spring. *Demand up?* Ask more. *Demand down?* Ask less (or wait till spring to post it).

- **Convertibles** – These are fun cars to drive. It's best to sell them when romance and merriment are in the air. As you can guess, that's spring and summer.

- **Supply and demand** – How many cars of your specific make and model are listed online in your area? If you own a Ford E-350 van and they are in short supply, cast your line at the high end to see if buyers will bite.

- **Unique vehicles** – Are you selling a rare or unique vehicle like the Honda Prelude or the Civic Si Mugen? Start the price on the high end, and hold it there longer before reducing it. Note on unique vehicles: Get the word out to as wide a range of markets as possible in order to increase the size of your buyer pool.

Unique Vehicles

This is one situation that I recommend www.eBayMotors.com as a place to market, because your vehicle will be visible to potential buyers across the country. With relatively low shipping costs available, unique or rare vehicles tend to do well on eBay.

Old School vs. New Rules

This brings us to one of the differences between Old School marketing of pre-owned cars and the New Rules. Both dealers and private sellers used to get away with keeping the price of their used vehicles artificially high while they waited for the "right" buyer to show up. Then two things happened:

1. The economy collapsed. First the housing market crumbled, followed by the financial industry which floats the loans for new and used vehicle sales. When financing dried up, sales of both new and used cars plummeted. However, the used-car market has recently rebounded. This has resulted in stronger demand and prices for may pre-owned vehicles.

2. The Internet entered every living room, library and coffee shop, changing how new and used cars are priced. Now *everyone* has access to the same information, so if your price is not competitive, you are not in the game.

As a result of this tumultuous change in the marketplace, a new phenomenon is emerging: instead of prices following a predictable path, explosive change can now send prices crashing far below the bottom of a predicted range. Or, as we have recently experienced, well above what anyone expected.

Fair Market Value

Potential volatile price fluctuations are
another reason to look at *fair market value* **now.**

KBB also revalues used cars weekly,
and those prices generally go down, not up.

Learn from the pros and get what you can today,
or there is a chance the market will shift unexpectedly,
leaving you holding a heavy set of keys tomorrow.

Setting an Initial Selling Price

Insert the figures on your car in this chart:

Used Car Price Range

KBB Suggested Retail Value $_____

Your Initial Selling Price $_____

KBB Private Party Value $_____

Following an Example in Real Time

My family has outgrown our 2006 Honda Civic LX sedan with automatic transmission and 36,000 miles. I'm in the San Francisco Bay Area market.

KBB's Suggested Retail Value is $15,845. I checked a bunch of other Internet sites. The best price was $15,900. Very close, so I'll use $15,845 as the high figure of my price range.

I know from experience that I won't get the dealer's full asking price. KBB says I will probably get between $12,845 for Good condition and $13,645 for Excellent. If I had a lot of time and didn't mind expending the effort, I'd use the highest possible Initial Selling Price to test the waters. The mileage on my Civic is less than most on the market, and the condition is at least as good.

Next, I check Craigslist, Kijiji, Oodle, AutoTrader, and Cars.com where I discover that most comparable private party vehicles are selling for $13,000 to $13,500. This tells me that the KBB figures I used to determine my price range is probably an accurate reflection of the current market here.

I'm going to hope that someone is willing to pay extra for low mileage and the extra effort I put into detailing the car, so I'll set my Initial Selling Price at $14,450. It's probably higher than most folks want to pay, but let's see if I get lucky.

My Used Car Price Range

KBB Suggested Retail Value $15,845

My Initial Selling Price $14,450

KBB Private Party Value $12,845

A Real World Test

Now that you know how to (1) find the price range and (2) determine the Initial Selling Price, let's hit the electronic pavement.

Test Your Starting Price

Why pay for a listing on a premium third-party website before you know if your price is reasonable? It's generally better to post at the Initial Selling Price on free websites. Remember that if it doesn't sell at the Initial Selling Price, we lower the price until the market starts nibbling at our line. If it's urgent to complete the sale, you can begin lowering your price after a few days.

You will be able to determine how reasonable your price is by the number and quality of responses you receive. Lower the price at a rate that you're comfortable with, given your circumstances.

Remember, too, that like Fred, your vehicle may sell on a free classified website before you make the move to a fee-based premium site. The possibility of making more on the sale depends on the effective use of free sites.

Insider Information — Timing is everything!

I discovered something interesting in the year I spent helping
develop my dealership's online marketing system.
Car buyers tend to shop in weekly cycles.

In the San Francisco Bay Area, interest in online postings
significantly increases on Wednesday afternoon
and remains high through Saturday morning.

Shoppers are lining up the cars they want to look at over the
weekend. Saturday is the biggest car shopping day of the week.

Once I became aware of this cycle, our marketing team tried to have all used car listings posted online by Wednesday morning. They began lowering prices the following Tuesday for selected vehicles that were still on the lot.

As a private seller, Tuesday should be your day to both post online AND make any price changes. This aligns with the natural shopping cycle of online car, truck, and SUV buyers.

Selling My Car

Back to my Honda Civic: my Initial Selling Price is $14,450. I don't get any calls the first week. This tells me that the price is too high, and I know from experience that there isn't much point in leaving it there.

The following Tuesday I lower the price to $14,150. Over the next week I get two calls, but no one is interested enough at that price to come over to see it.

The following Tuesday I lower the price to $13,900 and from four calls, one person comes over to take a look. This response tells me I've arrived at a reasonable price.

I can try to save money by continuing to list it only on free websites, or I can begin listing it with third-party websites such as Cars.com and AutoTrader.com. I'll have to pay for their service, but I know it is going to greatly expand the number of people who see my listing.

However, I didn't waste money listing there at the higher price that didn't attract any buyers.

The next week I continue to get calls from people wanting to test drive my car. It sells for $13,700, which is what I was hoping for, based on my research.

I could have sold it quicker had I used a lower
Initial Selling Price and immediately posted
it on premium third-party websites.

However, I took the extra time to see if there was a prospective buyer who was in a big enough rush to pay the Initial Selling Price. Sometimes there is.

In the end, I probably made a few hundred dollars extra by pricing it the way I did. Only you can decide what price and timetable is appropriate for your situation.

The Price Is Right

Pricing used cars is always a challenge,
yet critically important for both dealers and private sellers.

What about you?

I suggest that you do what dealers do:
use your intuition and market research, make your best guess,
and be ready to change your price based on results.

4

Setting Yourself Apart

Use Your Natural Advantage when Competing Against Dealers

I recently learned that one out of every five retail dollars feeds the automotive industry! (Or did until 2008 . . .)

The retail car business in particular is a key component of the economic engine that drives this country's economy. Yet despite a dealer's money, staff, advertising, and effort, *you the private seller* can grab the steering wheel in two key areas, when selling your used car online, because:

- Dealers are frozen in the old school mentality.

- A car dealer can't tell a personalized story about each vehicle they try to sell (though they've been known to make up a few).

The NEW RULES for Selling Cars

Many dealers have not noticed there are new rules for online marketing. Their problem is not just changing from traditional print-based marketing to the swifter currents of the Internet. They might as well be asleep on the beach with their old school approach when they work with customers.

Old School Approach

During my dealership career in Internet Sales, I listened closely to my customer's intense, even harsh, opinions about car dealers.

Guess what? Their intensity was an appropriate reaction to the old school approach. It's a self-inflicted wound that requires a huge amount of effort for the industry to unlearn. It's even difficult for them to openly discuss it.

Despite the price tag, buying a new or used vehicle is often an "impulse" purchase. A potential buyer walks onto the sales lot, discovers a vehicle they like, and may buy it on the spot.

Experienced salespeople are skilled in aggressively pushing their customers—including the impulse buyer—to close the sale **NOW**. There may be smiles up front, but customers intuitively know when something fishy is lurking beneath the surface. Few people are fooled for long.

Truly **professional** salespeople understand that if they push too hard, after emotions settle and the customer realizes what happened, resentment will leave a bad taste about the transaction.

And they'll remember it every time they crank the ignition or make their monthly payment. No wonder the public is cynical about car dealers.

Fool me once, shame on you.
Fool me twice, shame on me!

My customer's reaction to such crass manipulation was fast and furious when they felt they had no choice but to deal with a major car dealer again.

Be Real!

From my customers I discovered the two qualities they look for in their salesperson and their dealership:

- transparency
- authenticity

My customers desperately wanted to work with **real people**, salespeople who were upfront and honest. No seller-spin. No dealer-spin.

So here is where **you** benefit. Dealers are hampered by the daunting weight of an industry-wide negative image. You aren't. As a private seller you can *set yourself apart* from dealers by the way you present your vehicle in your online ad.

What I Learned

Here's what I learned from folks who bought cars and trucks from me:

Shun old school selling tactics.
Be honest, upfront, and transparent.

The way you communicate honesty and transparency to prospective online buyers is by presenting a clear, informative, and personable ad.

No gimmicks. No tricks. And above all, no bullshit.

Want to see an example of old school marketing that has been transferred to online ads? Go to Craigslist and AutoTrader and look at dealers' descriptions of the cars they are offering for sale.

They are condensed, boring, and ineffective (dare I say **impotent**). They can't turn online buyers on, which, lest we forget, is one of the main reasons for advertising!

Here are some lame dealer phrases I found in a six and a half minute search of local Craigslist postings:

- It runs as good as it looks.
- It is ready to drive home.
- You can't beat this price.
- Picture yourself driving it down the freeway.
- Don't spend more for less.
- Looks and runs like a car half its age.
- This is the car for you.

Feeble seller-spin! in a world where the New Rules of marketing dictate being direct, clear, and above all, specific. It's the difference between living up to the unpleasant stereotype versus being authentic and providing useful information that will help a buyer make the best decision for their need.

Don't bore your reader with drivel.
Avoid cheesy. Be simple. Be specific. Be real.

Personalizing is POWER!

The second advantage you have over most dealers is **personalization**. Dealers can have a hundred or more used cars clogging up their lot. This compares to just one for you. So you have the luxury of adding personal details, while most dealers don't have the experience, time, or resources to create a personalized ad for each vehicle in their inventory.

If you write a clear, personal, and informative online ad for a car that is appropriately priced and includes effective pictures, you are setting yourself apart from the crowd of online posters.

You will grab readers' attention, building a bond based on your authenticity—which increases the likelihood of your phone ringing. That's your best competitive weapon.

So Why Do People Shop at Major Car Dealers?

If my customers hated dealing with car dealers so much, why were they at the dealership talking to me in the first place?

It's fear that drives most people to a major dealer rather than risk buying from a small independent sales lot or an unknown individual who may not be trustworthy. It comes down to:

Better the devil you know than the one you don't.

What's the Risk? My customers told me that if they made a serious mistake, it would not only waste money, but it could negatively impact their lifestyle, their credit rating, and even their ability to work. No joking matter.

Practical Solutions

So private sellers need to understand the issues that shoppers face.

They need to adjust their selling approach to include, where possible, practical solutions to very real concerns.

Four Key Reasons

Most of my customers were happy to tell me why they disliked buying cars from private sellers or small independent car lots. It came down to these four concerns:

- **Mechanical** – Not understanding the mechanical aspect of cars. They were afraid they'd buy a car with a serious defect that *they* would have to fix.

- **Time** – The time and effort to look online, make calls, create a short list of vehicle to see in person, schedule test drives, schedule mechanical inspections, and more.

- **Financing** – They needed a loan. Dealing with a bank or credit union is a whole new set of problems.

- **Paperwork** – How do you draw up a bill of sale? What about the title? What if there is a loan on the car? What paperwork needs to be filled out at the DMV? Do you have to go there in person?

Major auto dealers provide these important services. Most of all, they help resolve *all* the above fears with one-stop shopping convenience:

- **Mechanical** – Their mechanics inspect all pre-owned vehicles and they boast that they have fixed any deficiencies. (Psst. . . you know you can only trust this if they offer a written guarantee, don't you?)

- **Time** – They offer (or have access to) a wide selection of vehicles. Customers may be able to find the vehicle they want by stopping at just one dealership. Also, they can test drive as many vehicles they want, right there, safely.

- **Financing** – The dealer completes credit applications on the spot, and works hard for instant approval.

- **Paperwork** – They complete all the paperwork and save their customers a trip to the DMV.

Those are real benefits! With a major dealer, a buyer can walk onto their lot and in a few hours literally drive away in their pre-owned vehicle.

If someone has questionable credit, little free time, no inclination to learn about mechanical issues, let alone figure out the paperwork, it would make sense to put up with the hassles of a dealer.

They would have to figure out all of this stuff for themselves if they ventured onto Craigslist and bought from a private seller.

How are You Gonna Compete with That?

Let's look at the major concerns again to see how you can alleviate the natural fears about buying from a private seller.

Mechanical

- Have the car detailed (see Chapter 2) so the buyer can see everything, from the spare tire and tools in the trunk, to the engine's belts and hoses under the hood.

- Show that your vehicle is road worthy. Say in your ad that you will provide:

  - a vehicle history report. You'll advance to the head of the class if you have it in electronic form to email a serious buyer (offer a hard copy when they come to test drive).

  - as many service records as possible, including the long, detailed work orders that show all work completed, and costs.

- Have you had one mechanic work on your car since you bought it? Or during the recent past? Then your mechanic is the best third-party expert a buyer can talk to.

    - Check with your mechanic before posting your car for sale: is it okay to give their name, work address, and telephone number as a referral? (Mechanics normally love this because chances are you are driving future business their way.)

    - Invite a buyer to call your mechanic for a first-hand description of the mechanical worthiness. Remind them that they can ask any questions they want—and that if *you* weren't 100% confident in the reliability of your car, you wouldn't be giving out your mechanic's number! Many customers are "sold" with just the offer, and will never actually call. Some will.

- Has a major dealer performed all your service work? This works in your favor, too. Have the business card of the service writer with you. Talk to the service writer ahead of time and let them know you will be referring potential buyers (and customers) their way.

    Service writers love this because they are paid a commission on all service orders that they write (thus, the name "service writer").

- Have your mechanic prepare a pre-purchase inspection report. (Don't be shy about asking your mechanic for a discount. They could be getting a long term customer out of the deal.) This is a huge confidence builder, and adds value to your car because you are saving buyers the bother and cost of arranging their own report.

- Don't have a regular mechanic? See my **Tools** page at www.BayAreaCarGuy.com/tools to find out how to get a standardized pre-purchase inspection performed by a national company through local mechanics.

Time

- Demonstrate that you are a "competent" seller by presenting a detailed and personable ad that includes effective pictures. Your ad will stand out and inspire confidence.

- A video walk-around is a cool tool, and it's also a time saver for potential buyers. They can see your car without making a (possibly useless) trip. This sets you apart, builds trust, and acknowledges that you respect your buyer's needs. In the majority of cases, if a buyer comes to see the car after viewing the video, they're ready to buy it.

- After discussing the details of the car itself, let them know that you're prepared to move forward quickly. Offer them the paperwork, from service records to the vehicle history report. Let them know if the title is "free and clear," and if you have it with you.

- If there is a bank loan registered against the title (meaning it's *not* clear of all liens), assure them that you already know the simplest way to handle the payoff procedure. Offer to email them a copy of the bill of sale you plan to use (see Chapter 12).

- A simple, yet effective suggestion is to meet the buyer halfway for the test drive. They'll appreciate your effort to help them. You'll stand out from other sellers. Read Chapter 11 about the safeguards for meeting in person.

Paperwork

- In chapter 12, you will learn how to deal with the bill of sale, DMV, and bank loans. Showing a prospective buyer that you are familiar with what needs to be done is another way to build trust.

Who You Gonna Call?

Not sure who to deal with for pre-purchase inspection reports, getting your car detailed or service work done? Find resources that can help you now on my **Tools** page at www.BayAreaCarGuy.com/tools.

It's tough enough getting everything done when selling your car online. You can at least find out who is recommended (and who is not) BEFORE you make an appointment.

Fast & Furious

The car business is fast-paced and ever-changing.

The vast majority of used car buyers now begin their vehicle search online, so learn to make your online ad as effective as possible.

This natural advantage sets you apart from typical private sellers and old school dealers.

5

Marketing for Free **PART I**

Craigslist: Try What's Free
Before You Pay for Premium Websites

Unless you're in a hurry or don't have to worry about a budget, list your vehicle on free websites before going premium. However, if it's critical to sell your car quickly, post it on every website immediately. But don't think that ***premium*** is necessarily better than *free*.

In some markets, free sites such as Craigslist, Backpage, Oodle, or Kijiji are at least as effective. Since each local market is different, find out what works best in your area.

For most people, it's best to begin with free classified sites to establish a reasonable selling price (see how to price your vehicle in Chapter 3) before moving onto premium websites that charge a fee or commission for their services.

Let's begin with www.craigslist.org

In most markets, Craigslist is the largest online
classified website available. If Craigslist isn't the largest
and most effective one where you live, then use what is.

The next chapter (Chapter 6) offers help for discovering which free websites to use. Better yet, use all the free websites that are active in your area. What the heck: they're free, and the more exposure, the better. Right?

Before we get to the details of how to produce an effective online ad, you'll need a personal Craigslist account. Signing up is easy. Begin at www.craigslist.org.

How a Prospective Buyer Uses Craigslist

It's important to see what your "quarry" will be searching. Knowing how your ad will look once it's posted will help in designing it to sell effectively.

- Open Craigslist (no need to log in)

- Under **for sale** click **cars+trucks**

- Here are a few typical listings:

  - **1996 Pontiac Sunfire - Mechanics Special, $650,** (emeryville) img **owner**

  - **2004 Nissan 350z TOURING ** CLEAN MUST SEE, $14985,** (fremont / union city / newark) img **dealer**

  What you see is: Year, Make, Model, some phrase to make it seem special, followed by specific location, "**img**" if there are photos, and posting category (by **owner** or by **dealer**)

- When you click this title, the ad itself appears. At the top is this title and price. Followed by:

  - Reply to: **sale-5edta-1215896459@craigslist.org** – This is an anonymized email address.

  - **Date: 2009-06-10, 9:58PM PDT** – This tells the date and time of the posting.

You'll find the information the seller thought was important for you to know about the vehicle, and perhaps some photos.

Listing Your Item for Sale

Listing your ad on Craigslist is also easy. Be sure to list your posting under **cars & trucks - owner** instead of **dealer**. And provide as precise a location as Craigslist will allow.

Important Posting Boxes

Here are the specific boxes that require information.

- **Posting Title** – This is the first tidbit of information a prospective buyers sees about your vehicle. Unfortunately, they see *your* Title along with hundreds of others, which means your words need to grab their attention or they'll pass you by. We'll get to that shortly.

- **Price** – If you don't price your vehicle correctly, you'll either "leave money on the table" by pricing it too low, or no one will contact you because it's priced too high. Read about the **Initial Selling Price** and how to price your vehicle in Chapter 3.

- **Specific Location** – If this box is active, you are required to narrow down your location. For example, if you list your vehicle in the Houston area and you live in Bellaire, type **Bellaire** in the Specific Location box if a pull down menu with the exact location is not available.

- **Reply to** – This protects your privacy. Choose "anonymize" in order to hide your actual email address. A buyer can send email to the coded address (for example: Reply to: **sale-rv36q-1217510735@ craigslist.org**) and Craigslist forwards it to your email. If you will not be checking your email, choose "hide." This eliminates any email option. You'll need to give another way to contact you. (You want to be easily reached, because a shopper is not going to wait for you to get home from work to return their call, given all the competitive listings.)

- **Post Description** – The content you include here will either motivate buyers to contact you—or not. Content is king. Good news: I've included a template that you can copy into the Post Description box, so it's simple for you to insert your vehicle's specifics. The template ensures that all necessary information is included.

- **Add / Edit Images** – Using pictures that clearly and accurately represent your car will separate your ad from average and sub-par postings. In Chapter 9, discover how to take pictures that SELL your vehicle.

Let's Get to It — Content is KING!

Now you get to create an effective post that motivates prospective buyers to contact *you* first! This is where your content stands out from the hundreds of other listings vying for attention.

It should make a buyer say, "Hey, Maggie, this is just the car I've been looking for! It's even bright red like I've been wanting!"

The Posting Title

The Posting Title is the first information that buyers see. It must make your listing distinctive. Year, make and model first, then note the extra features that make it special.

Each free classified website allows a different number of characters for the **Title** line. Craigslist offers 70 characters. This is the first glance, so use as much of this allotment as possible.

There are two parts to the Posting Title:

1. **Begin with the Basics** – Always start with the year, make, model, and trim level, followed by other specific manufacturer's descriptors of your model of car, truck, or SUV. Here are a couple of examples:

   – 2006 Honda Civic EX-L Coupe –

   – 2008 Ford F-250 XLT SuperDuty Cabela's Package –

2. **Followed by the Extras** – What sets your vehicle apart from similar vehicles being offered for sale? If it has fewer miles, include the exact mileage—but only if that is a key selling feature.

   What else to include? Check my Top Ten Key Words list in Chapter 8—these are the features that matter most buyers. If your vehicle can boast any of those features, NAME THEM!

   When I was posting hundreds of listings online each month, these Top Ten Key Words set my phone ringing. You'll put some of them in CAPS in the Posting Title since these are the features most buyers value. If you have characters to spare, use key words from the primary Buying Criteria, also in Chapter 8.

Don't Crowd the Listing

Despite what others recommend, there are times when it is preferable to use ALL CAPS in your post. When used sparingly, ALL CAPS create a visual separation between words AND phrases.

I also like to use a hyphen ("-") or a longer dash ("—") with a space on each side to further separate key words and phrases. These formatting techniques make the Posting Title easier to read and allow key words to stand out, increasing their effectiveness.

This is how Posting Titles should look once you add the extras:

- 2006 Honda Civic EX-L Coupe - LEATHER - Moonroof - Extended Warranty

- 2008 Ford F-250 XLT SuperDuty Cabela's Package - 4X4 - TOW - Leather

To Sum Up

You want the first half of the Posting Title to cover the basics,
then list extras that make your vehicle special.

Create a spacious look, while including maximum features.

The **Posting Title** must entice shoppers to click for more information
and you do that by listing the features and benefits they want.

Posting the Vehicle Description

Clicking on the **Posting Title** takes your buyer to the Vehicle Description. What you say here must persuade an interested buyer to contact you for more information, and to hopefully buy your car. Make it simple, sharp, and accurate.

There are three parts to the Vehicle Description. Let's take a quick look at each before we begin the creative process of building your specific content:

1. **Description Title** – This is similar to the second half of the Posting Title. It's valuable to repeat the positive in an online ad. Include the major features from the Top Ten Key Words list and the Buying Criteria, OR use a simple headline to grab the reader's attention.

2. **Personalized Description of the Vehicle** – Describe the good, the bad, and the ugly. However, you can also tell a story to give real life descriptions of the positive aspects of your car.

3. **Itemized Vehicle Details** – Because of the importance of this section, I've designed a template so you won't miss any vital details.

Now let's build the content that will help *your* vehicle sell fast!

Description Title

Use one of two styles, depending on how many features your car has, and how much personalizing you are able to include.

1. **Features-Style Title** – If you can, include at least four features from the Top Ten Key Words and Buying Criteria in Chapter 8.

    Use ALL CAPS with a "space - hyphen - space" between them. This format grabs the readers attention and guides their focus to your personalized content. Here's an example:

- **1-OWNER - LEATHER - MOON ROOF - ALLOY WHEELS - 36 M-P-G - LOW MILES** -- We bought this Honda Civic because of the great gas mileage ... (continue with your personal description of the vehicle).

2. **Headline-Style Title** – Use this style if there are not enough effective key words or buying criteria that apply to your vehicle. Make a bold statement with a SINGLE THEME.

   Check these out:

   - **1-OWNER VEHICLE WITH ULTRA LOW MILES** — The mileage is not a misprint - just 3,461! We bought this car...

   - **36 M-P-G - WHAT A GREAT COMMUTER CAR!** -- I have saved so much money on gas since buying this....

   - **BASIC WORK TRUCK WITH 4-WHEEL DRIVE** — Nothing fancy. This tough work truck has more than paid for itself over the 2-years that I've owned it...

You're grabbing the reader's attention! This ALL CAPS title leads directly to your personalized description, where the real selling takes place.

Personalize – Personalize – Personalize

This is the one area that will separate you from competing listings.

Beyond powerful descriptive phrases, you can build rapport with a reader based on your personal knowledge and history with the car.

Personalized Description

You also alleviate their fears about buying from a private seller if you can engage them in your story. Include:

- Why you bought this car in the first place
- What you most enjoy about it
- Why you are selling it

Note what is unique about your relationship to your vehicle, and why that may be important to the next owner. Use a conversational tone.

- **Which features initially attracted you to this vehicle?**

  I bought "Miss G." as we call her, for the great gas mileage. She's saved us a ton of money over the last two years!

- **What features you like the most, and why?**

  At first I didn't think I would even use the heated seats. But after one cold winter, I'll never get another car without them.

- **What features you use the most and why?**

  My kids love the DVD rear entertainment system, and I love the peace I get on long trips. No more fighting and arguing. I'd never get another van without one.

- **How well it has served you and your family?**

  I'm a typical soccer mom, driving my kids—and most of the neighbors' kids—to music lessons, sports practice and mall distractions. Having an 8-seater van with power sliding doors has made life so much easier over the last three years.

- **Have you recommended this vehicle to family or friends?**

  My sister and one cousin have bought the same model based on my recommendation. They love it!

- **If appropriate, why you are selling?**

  This van has served me and my family so well, I'll miss it. But we're moving to the country where we need a 4-wheel drive.

Below are actual **Title** and **Personalized Descriptions** that I helped customers create for Craigslist.

Remember Fred whose problem started this book? Here's his posting:

D-V-D - 3RD ROW SEATING - LEATHER - MOON ROOF - 4 HEATED SEATS - POWER FRONT SEATS - DRIVER'S MEMORY SEAT - RUNNING BOARDS - BACKUP SENSORS - TOW PACKAGE - TINTED WINDOWS - 22-INCH GIO CHROME EXTRA WIDE WHEELS -- I bought this low mileage Escalade as a GM Certified Used Vehicle in the fall of 2007. Because it was certified, it met a higher standard and came with an extended warranty that will continue until the fall of this year. I have kept it fully serviced and it's ready for the next owner.

I love this Escalade because of all the room, the DVD entertainment system with 2 wireless headsets, and all the upgraded features – it has so many, I'll probably forget to list them all. I've got the CARFAX report which shows no problems. Email your questions or call Fred at 510-648-0000.

I wrote this ad for a family moving back to France after the economy collapsed:

1-OWNER - LOW MILES - MOON ROOF - TOW PACKAGE - ALLOY WHEELS - LOTS OF WARRANTY REMAINING -- We bought this Nissan Rogue because we love a spacious interior and great gas mileage - 27 M-P-G. We decided not to pay $1000 extra for AWD, since we don't need it where we live – and it saves on gas. With 2 small kids, SAFETY was our big concern - 6 air bags, including full-length side curtain air bags, active front head restraints, dynamic stability control, traction control, near-perfect crash test rating, and 4-wheel ABS brakes. It's been the perfect urban family SUV.

I have lots more pictures—just ask. They show this Rogue is still in great condition—though there are a few scratches and a couple of small dents on the bumper. We just did the 15k service which included replacing the oil and filter. Contact Jenny at 510-648-0000.

How do you describe a vehicle with almost no miles? See below:

THE MILES ARE NOT A MISPRINT -- Just 3,971 miles on this 2008 xD! Even though we love this Scion, we rarely take her out. We now have to down-size and that means this great little car is for sale. She's in near-perfect condition!

WHY DO WE LOVE HER? -- This cherry red xB is not only fun to drive, but she has a great sound system with an iPod connector (I'm including the connector cord with the car). The AM/FM/CD plays WMA & MP3 files that I burn from my laptop. She also has Advanced Audio Coding (AAC) and is Satellite-ready. Good design: the audio controls are on the steering wheel: not merely convenient, but SAFER. This RED xB not only looks cool and gets great gas mileage - 28 mpg - but she has important SAFETY FEATURES - from ABS brakes and traction control to full-length side curtain air bags, and a near-perfect crash test rating. She's also got air/cruise/tilt and power windows/locks/side-mirrors. (We call her "MM" after Ms. Monroe in her shockingly tight red skirt in *Niagara!*)

I have lots more pictures. They show the great condition this Scion is in - and would you expect anything less with almost no miles on this Sports Wagon! When you test drive her, I'll point out the few exterior scratches because they're hardly noticeable. There are so few miles, she's never been service. Call Arthur at 510-648-0000.

Itemized Vehicle Details

This is the comprehensive list at the end of your post. It's the information a buyer looks at to confirm that the basic vehicle fits their needs.

The VIN is included, in case a buyer wants to purchase their own vehicle history report. Price and contact information are essential at the end.

If the "Pictures," "Clear Title?" or "Video Walk-Around Available?" lines don't apply, delete them, along with any other lines that are not applicable.

Craigslist Template

The **entire** template below can be copied into the Vehicle Description. I have included sample content to give you an idea how the post should look when finished. You can simply replace my sample information in *italics* with information specific to your vehicle. Text in "bold" stays in the ad.

Better yet, go to www.BayAreaCarGuy.com/tools and look under the Craigslist heading to copy a blank template directly into your craigslist ad. Simply add the specific information about your vehicle. This is just a small part of the useful and free information that I provide on my website.

\<b\> 1-OWNER - LOW MILES - MOON ROOF - TOW PACKAGE - ALLOY WHEELS - LOTS OF WARRANTY REMAINING \</b\> -- *We bought this 2-wheel drive Nissan Rogue because we love a spacious interior and great gas mileage - 27 M-P-G. We decided not to pay $1000 extra for AWD, since we don't need it where we live – and it saves on gas. With 2 small kids, SAFETY was our big concern – 6 air bags, including full-length side curtain air bags, active front head restraints, dynamic stability control, traction control, near-perfect crash test rating, and 4-wheel ABS brakes. It's been the perfect urban family SUV.*

I have lots more pictures - just ask. They show this Rogue is still in great condition

– though there are a few scratches and a couple of small dents on the bumper. We just did the 15k service which included replacing the oil and filter. Contact Jenny at 510-648-0000.

Here are the vehicle details:

Year – *2008*
Make – *Nissan*
Model – *Rogue S*
VIN – *JN8AS58T48W01369*
Miles – *16,441*
Body Style – *SUV*
Engine – *2.5L, 4 cyl*
Transmission – *CVT – Automatic*
Drivetrain – *FWD*
Exterior Color – *Silver*
Interior Color – *Black*
Gas Mileage – *22 mpg/city, 27 mpg/hwy*
Vehicle History Report Available – Yes
Video Walk-Around Available – Yes (ask me to send you a link)
Clear Title? – Yes
Pictures – More available, just ask.
Price – *$16,950.00*
Contact – *Call Phyllis at 510-648-0000 or click on the email link.*

Finishing Up

- Click **Add/Edit Images** to include photos in your ad. See Chapter 9 to learn how to take pictures of your car.

- Always upload the Primary Exterior Photo first. After you have uploaded the pictures and finalized the text, click **Continue** at the bottom of the page.

- You are presented with a preview of the finished ad. If you want to change anything click **Edit** at the bottom, otherwise click **Continue**.

- After entering the dancing verification words on the challenge screen (the correct technical term is captcha) click **Continue** and you are done.

Congratulation! You posted your Craigslist ad.

Repost as Needed

After the current posting expires (7 to 45 days after initially posting it, depending on your location), **login** again at the upper-right corner of Craiglist's home page.

You'll see your expired ad with a contrasting colored background:

- Click on the title, then **Repost this Posting**. You have to repeat some of the initial categories, including **Car & truck – by owner**, followed by your location.

- Make any needed changes to your ad, including lowering the price if appropriate, and click **Add/Edit Images**. You need to add images every time you repost. You can use this opportunity to put up different pictures, but always upload the Primary Exterior Photo first.

- Click **Continue** at the bottom of the page. You are presented with a preview of the finished ad. If you want to change anything click **Edit** at the bottom, otherwise click **Continue**. After entering dancing verification words click **Continue** and you are done.

HTML Enhancements

Experimenting with new strategies can be fun AND can increase the effectiveness of your ad.

If you're adventurous, you can customize and format your content with simple HTML code. Craigslist is one of the websites that requires the use of HTML code to add additional formatting to your text.

You may want to make your Title in the Vehicle Description area bold so it stands out even more (already done in the template above). You'll need HTML code to do that. Go to the **Tools** page of my website at www.BayAreaCarGuy. com/tools for a list of HTML code that Craigslist has identified as working well with their system.

Need HELP?

I offer two levels of support to private sellers who feel they could use a little help with their online ad. The **Quick Consult** and **Write My Ad** are available on my **Need Help**? page at BayAreaCarGuy.com. Car dealers can look on the **Dealers** page for support available to them.

Marketing for Free   PART II

Craigslist - Kijiji - Oodle - Backpage

Craigslist is the towering giant among free online classified websites. 50 million unique visitors regularly land on Craigslist each month. Craigslist is the 8th largest website in the US, and the 24th largest in the world. But don't snear at using Backpage, Kijiji, and Oodle, each of which had between 2 and 3 million visitors.

Does this mean you should rush out and post your sedan only on Craigslist? That depends on where you live. Classified websites are designed to offer a local approach for selling to local buyers.

For example, according to recent statistics Craigslist is not the top site in all markets. If you live in New York City, Washington, DC, or Las Vegas, post on Kijiji first, then Craigslist.

However, St. Louis and Houston residents primarily post to Kijiji, with Oodle next. In these cities Craigslist comes in a distant third. For San Diego and Portland, Oregon, Craigslist is used more than others, but Oodle easily beats out Kijiji for second place.

Where to Begin?

With classified websites organized to provide a local service, how do you determine which free website is best for selling your car?

The popularity of free classified sites changes quickly. See the end of this chapter for ideas on how to find the most popular free sites in your area.

Post on as Many Websites as Possible

What the heck, they're free, right?
You'll only be out the time it takes to create each post.

However, by checking the popularity of free websites in your area,
you'll at least know which ones to begin with
if you can't post your vehicle on all of them right away.

In Chapter 5, we took an in-depth look at how to post your vehicle on Craigslist. We'll use that foundation for the remaining three websites described in this chapter.

Kijiji.com — Animal? Vegetable? Or Mineral?

Kijiji is Swahili for "village." If you believe corporate-speak, it's named to reflect the sense of community that develops as its members exchange goods, services, and ideas.

$$K-i-j-i-j-i$$
Pronounce it: kee-gee-gee

Even though learning the pronunciation—as well as keying in the name—may take a bit of getting used to, the Kijiji website is one of the easiest to navigate when posting an ad.

Begin by Going to www.kijiji.com

- On the homepage pick your locale

- Click the **Free - Post your free ad** tab at the top of the page.

- There is a separate **Cars & vehicles** section. Choose a specific category: probably **Cars** or **Trucks, vans, SUVs.** This takes you to the **Create Your Ad** page.

You can literally copy and paste the Title and Vehicle Description information from Craigslist to Kijiji with one exception (see below). The following are the major differences between Kijiji to Craigslist:

- The Title line allows only 64 characters, so you may have to shorten your Craigslist title from 70.

- You can post eight pictures instead of four. Take full advantage of this benefit.

- All ads in the vehicle section expire after 60 days.

One advantage of Kijiji is you can design a distinctive ad with its formatting toolbar that looks like MS Word's. Choose font and size, bold/italic, bullets, colors for letters and background. You can even add horizontal bars to frame parts of your content.

When you have completed the **Create Your Ad** page, click **Preview** at the bottom. You can make as many revisions as needed before clicking **Post Your Ad.**

Let Your Creativity Loose

Make your ad distinctive, but keep it simple—
the *essential* information is what buyers are looking for.

Managing Your Ad Is Simple

- Edit information in your post—including lowering the price if it doesn't sell immediately—by clicking the **Manage my ads** link at the top of the page.

- Remember to delete the ad if your vehicle sells—you don't want to waste the buyer's time, nor get needless phone calls at work.

Oodle — And Now for Something Completely Different

While Kijiji is modeled closely after Craigslist, Oodle is not as straight forward. Oodle gathers classified ads from thousands of websites (it boasts 80,000 different sources), then turns around and feeds those ads to the hundreds of websites in its network.

The good news for you, the private seller, is that your Oodle ad shows up on websites like Walmart Classifieds, as well as hundreds of other Oodle network members where you wouldn't think to post.

In the car business, we like to throw a lot of mud on the wall to see what sticks. Get your post up on as many websites as possible because you never know when some buyer will like your mud.

Begin by Going to www.oodle.com

- It's a good idea to **Register** (upper right corner) before posting your ad.

- When you get back to the Oodle home page click **Sign In** on the upper-right side.

- Now you can click **Free - Post Ad** in the upper-right corner.

- A simple **Post an Ad** pop-up page appears.

- Enter **Title, Neighborhood**. Under **Category**, choose **Vehicles**. It will expand for more details.

- Under **Subcategory**, choose **Cars**. This includes all highway vehicles except commercial trucks.

- Under 2nd Subcategory, select your vehicle's type.

You can copy and paste the Title and Vehicle Description information from Craigslist to Oodle. Here are some similarities and differences between the two:

- The number of characters you can insert in the Title line is the same: 70.

- Like Craigslist, Oodle allows you to post four pictures. Use all of them.

- All ads in the vehicle section last 30 days before you must renew.

Also like Craigslist, you can use simple HTML code in the vehicle description area to format your post. I suggest changing the Headline in the vehicle description area to **bold** font. Do this by adding "" at the beginning of the Headline and "" at the end.

Want to do More?

Go to the **Tools** page of my website at www.BayAreaCarGuy.com/tools for a list of HTML code that you can use to enhance your ad.

Fill in the remaining boxes that provide more vehicle information and click **Continue**. Complete **Step 2**, the verification page, and click **Post**. Unlike other sites, you need to **check your email to activate the ad.**

Managing Your Ad is Simple.

- Edit information in your post—including lowering the price if it doesn't sell immediately—by clicking **My Posted Ads** at the top of your home page once you have signed in.

- Remember to delete the ad if your vehicle sells—you don't want to waste the buyer's time, nor get needless phone calls at work.

Backpage — The Alternative Choice

I like working with Backpage because I have an affinity for my local San Francisco Bay Area alternative newsweekly.

Backpage is not only owned by the original alternative newspaper, New York's *Village Voice*, but your ad may be displayed along with classified ads from the back of various local alternative newspapers including my *SF Weekly* (San Franciso Bay Area), *LA Weekly* (Los Angeles), *City Pages* (Minneapolis), and *Seattle Weekly* (Seattle).

Backpage readers are nothing if not loyal. Once on Backpage, readers obviously enjoy surfing the site. Why obviously? Backpage is up to an incredible one-billion page views per month. This is a very good thing for sellers.

Backpage online ads are free. Yet you have the option of paying a fee to add your post to the local, printed newspaper, and for posting online in multiple cities.

Begin by Going to www.backpage.com

- At the very bottom of the home page click **Account Login** to create your account.

- Once you are signed in, on the upper-right you will see **Post new ad**, followed by a pull-down menu entitled, Choose metro area. Once you have chosen your locale click **Go**.

- Choose **Automotive** section, then **Autos for sale**.

You have arrived at **Step 1: Write Ad**. You can literally copy and paste the Title and Vehicle Description information from Craigslist to Backpage. These are the major differences:

- The Title line allows 100 characters, so you can add more features from the Top Ten Key Words list and Buying Criteria (Chapter 8).

- You can post four pictures. Use all of them.

- Ads remain online for 45 days before you have to renew.

Backpage has simplified the text formatting in the vehicle description area, so you can spruce up your post. There are three format buttons available: **Bold, Italic**, and **Underline**. As in MS Word, highlight the text that you'd like to format, then click the button to emphasize your text. The HTML code is added to the text right before your eyes.

Go to the **Tools** page of my website at www.BayAreaCarGuy.com/tools for a list of additional HTML code you can use to personalize your ad.

When complete, click **Continue** to be taken to **Step 2: Preview Ad**. You can either click **Edit Ad** to make changes, or type the verification word into the box, then click **Place Ad Now.** You are done. Your ad is live.

You can make changes to your ad—like lowering the price—through an email sent to you by Backpage. The subject line begins with Edit/Delete link, and includes a link that takes you to your post. That's also the way to delete it when your deal is complete.

A Never Ending Story

The Internet is endless. So are the number of websites for posting your vehicle. The sites listed here are the major ones used throughout the country, but are by no means the only ones.

Ask your friends, co-workers, and family which are the best sites, including if there are other local sites that you should use. Do a Google search using these search words:

<your city, state, or region> **free vehicle classified ads**.

For example, to search the Minneapolis area, type:

Minneapolis free vehicle classified ads.

Use the busiest websites that appear in your search results. Then do a search for the vehicle you are selling on the sites that made your short list. Post to the ones with the most traffic and the most specific listings of your car.

Remember the "Mud On The Wall" Theory?

Always throw up as much "mud" as you have time and energy for.

You never know when that last post on some
obscure website will generate a phone inquiry about your car.

But be smart: *begin with the largest, high-traffic sites in your area.*

7

Premium Websites

Posting Your Ad on AutoTrader and Cars.com

The two most popular premium websites are AutoTrader and Cars.com. At the dealership, I used both extensively. They are valuable both for the large number of people who look for vehicles there, and because they feed their listings to other popular sites.

This means that when you post your vehicle on one, you gain exposure on the others—at no additional charge.

AutoTrader is the larger of the two:

- In 2010 it logged over 14 million unique visitors a month.

- It hosts over 3 million new and used vehicles from both private sellers and 40,000 dealers.

- AutoTrader partners with MSN Autos and Edmunds.com, among others.

Cars.com is somewhat smaller, but reaches a different audience:

- It has about 10 million unique visitors each month.

- It hosts 2.5 million new and used vehicles from 15,000 dealers, and private sellers.

- It partners with 175 local newspapers and TV stations, as well as with USAToday.com and Yahoo Autos.

- Most auto dealers post their entire used car inventory on at least one—and often on both—websites.

What about YOUR Vehicle?

The growing success among dealers has become a challenge for private sellers using these services. Dealer listings show up at the front of search results because (1) of their vast numbers and (2) the fact that many dealers pay extra to be there (AutoTrader).

This can push your private posting so far back that it gets buried under their rubble. What to do? On AutoTrader you can pay the extra fee for a premium listing to appear closer to the top of search results.

So is it worth the extra cost to post your ad on premium sites? 26 million buyers are out there shopping on AutoTrader and Cars.com. Do you really want to miss the opportunity to sell to them? If you decide to go premium, should you use just one of these sites? Or pay for both?

Unfortunately, my crystal ball is broken, so there's no way to give you the correct answer to any of these questions in advance of actually getting your feet wet in the selling swamp.

What works for one person will not necessarily work for the next. It can be crazy-making, but in truth there are simply too many variables (see Chapter 3), like where you live and the type of car you are offering for sale.

Some private sellers swear by AutoTrader because they've had success there. Others will only list with Cars.com. Still others use only free websites.

That's why I suggested this strategy in Chapter 3:

> *If you NEED to sell your car NOW, or cost is not an issue,*
> *post your vehicle to every website possible.*

However, if you have the time, and/or a limited budget, begin with just the free sites to:

- make sure you have priced the vehicle correctly
- see if it will sell on a free classified site prior to paying for a premium service

Something to Learn?

There may be something for you to learn from the pros about where to post, since dealers have to juggle their limited advertising budgets. They run numbers, analyze results, and track sales in an effort to make sure that they are getting the biggest bang for their buck.

Even though there is no direct fee for using free sites, dealers still pay someone to create and post those ads, and these costs need to be factored in.

> *The more mud you throw on the wall,*
> *the greater the chance of some sticking.*

The more websites that carry your ad, the better the chance of someone seeing it, becoming interested, contacting you, test driving, and buying *your* car. Happy Days!

Part 1 — Creating Your Ad on AutoTrader.com

AutoTrader provides a great service, has some useful tools, and includes a user-friendly interface for creating your ad.

Go to www.autotrader.com. Near the top of the home page, on the third level down, click **Sell Your Car**. On the next page enter your **zip code** under **Get Started**.

Your credit card charge won't be processed until the very end, so play around with the different combinations until you get exactly what you want at a price that fits your budget.

There are two major differences between the four plans—the duration of the listing and the number of pictures that you can post.

Pricing Options

You are presented with a choice of 7 Day Trial ($0), Standard ($19), Enhanced ($39), or Deluxe ($59) packages. Remember, you get what you pay for—AND these fees are just the beginning. Later you will be offered extra features for additional cost, so don't be surprised.

There is one significant disadvantage with the 7-day free trial package: no thumbnail picture comes up in search results, which cuts your chance of someone clicking on your ad in half.

This leaves you two choices: move up to the Standard package, or pay the extra $10 for the thumbnail feature in the 7 Day Trial package (defeating the purpose of FREE).

Once you have chosen your plan (and remember, you can always go back and change this before you check out) you are taken to the **Ad Details** page. This is where you create your ad.

- To the right of the pull-down menus is the handy pricing tool. Use this to confirm the price you have already established. It also shows how many vehicles similar to yours are available.

- Remember that dealers sell their vehicles for more than private sellers. Refer back to Chapter 3 if you still have questions about pricing your vehicle.

- The pull-down menus on the top-left side of the page helps you input the specifications of your vehicle.

- Check all the options that apply to your vehicle. Take your time to make sure you don't miss any. If necessary, go out and look carefully at your car to confirm its actual features, or do a Google search of your make, model, and year to determine them.

  Completing this section accurately can make the difference between selling your car or not—or selling for its full value. For example, if a parent insists on side curtain air bags (added protection for their child), and you haven't checked this option, you are out of the running even if your vehicle has them. Also, a potential buyer will offer you less money if they aren't aware of all the features your car has.

The next section on the page is the **Online Ad Comments**. This is where you add the personalized comments that make your ad distinctive from all others. This is the place to shine since AutoTrader automatically creates the Title line, and lists the miles, price, and options.

Checking Out the Competition

Before you go on, check out the competition.
Open a new page in your web browser and again go to
www.autotrader.com.

Do a search for the vehicle you are selling to see what your listing is up against. See how dealers are presenting their vehicles, and compare those to the postings by private sellers.

For example, I did a search for a 2006 Honda Civic using my own San Francisco Bay Area zip code. It came up with 34 results. 10 of those did not have a picture of the car being sold.

A few had stock photos from the manufacturer—which is just as bad as having no picture at all. Those dealers knocked themselves out of the running by not posting a picture of their car. If you were a buyer would you click on their ad?

Then I counted dealers and private sellers. Only two were private, but both had pictures and personalized comments. Neither one did a great job of describing their car, but what they did post was head and shoulders above the dealers' efforts.

The majority of the dealer's descriptions were simply "VIN explosions"—the standard and extra features generated from the Vehicle Identification Number database. VIN explosions can be presented in two standard forms or in computer-generated sentences.

I have created what appears similar to all three examples. They are as follows:

Standard VIN Explosion – SHORT VERSION: 4-Cyl. 1.8L VTEC; Automatic; FWD; ABS (4Wheel); Air Conditioning; AlloyWheels; AM/FM Stereo; Cruise Control; DualFront Air Bags; FrontSide Air Bags; Moon Roof; Power Door Locks; Power Steering; Power Windows; Single Compact Disc; Tilt Wheel.

Standard VIN Explosion – LONG VERSION: Air Conditioning, Power Steering, Power Windows, Power Door Locks, Tilt Wheel, Cruise Control, AM/FM Stereo, MP3 (SingleCD), DualFront Air Bags, FrontSide Air Bags, ABS (4Wheel), Moon Roof, Rear Spoiler, Alloy Wheels, Control link MacPherson strut front suspension, Reactive link double wishbone rear suspension, Front/rear stabilizer bars, Power rack & pinion steering, Pwr ventilated front/solid rear disc brakes, Anti lock braking system (ABS) w/electronic brake distribution (EBD), 13.2 gallon fuel tank, Chrome exhaust finisher, Pwr moonroof w/1-touch feature, Impact-absorbing body-color bumpers, Body-color rear decklid spoiler, Multi-reflector halogen headlamps, Daytime running lights, Body-color pwr mirrors, Tinted glass, Variable intermittent windshield wipers, Body-color door handles, Front bucket seats w/reclining seatbacks adjustable head restraints, Passenger seat walk-in feature w/memory, 60/40 fold down rear seatback, Center console w/sliding armrest storage compartment, (2) 12V auxiliary pwr outlets, Coin tray, Front/rear beverage holders, Steering wheel-mounted audio & cruise controls, Tilt/telescoping steering column, Immobilizer theft-deterrent system, Blue backlit gauges-inc: tachometer, Digital odometer & (2) trip meters, Maintenance minder system, Outside temp indicator, Headlights-on reminder, Pwr door locks w/auto-lock feature, Security system w/remote entry trunk release, Cruise control, Remote fuel filler door release, Remote trunk release w/lock, Air conditioning w/micron filtration system, Rear window defroster w/timer, Integrated rear window antenna, Satin-finish door handle pulls, Door pocket storage bins, Dual visor vanity mirrors, Blue ambient console lighting, Map lights, Cargo area light, Rear seat garment hooks, Passenger side seatback pocket, Side curtain airbags, Front/rear 3-point seat belts w/front automatic tensioning system, Child safety seat anchors (LATCH), Emergency trunk release.

Enhanced VIN Explosion (with computer generated sentences): This 2006 Honda Civic 4-door EX Sedan features a 1.8L L4 MPI SOHC 16V 4 cyl Gasoline engine. It is equipped with a 5-speed automatic transmission. The vehicle is Electrolite Blue Pearl with a Grey Cloth interior. It is offered with the remaining factory warranty.

Hard On the Eyes?

Do your eyes begin to blur from
reading these mechanical descriptions?

Imagine a buyer sorting through online listings for an hour!
These postings quickly speed buyers along to the next listing.

Bad for dealers—good for you!

Getting It Right

Take another look at the search results. AutoTrader automatically inserts most of the content of the listing, including the Posting Title (year, make, model), as well as the mileage and price. After clicking on a specific listing, you'll see the details of the major features and options.

The only way you can make your listing stand out from these is by what you write in the **Online Ad Comments**. Here is where you beat out the dealers who use a VIN explosion. Your Headline must grab your buyer's attention and draw them to your personalized description.

Here are two examples of what your headline might look like:

- **1-OWNER - LEATHER - MOON ROOF - ALLOY WHEELS - 36 M-P-G - LOW MILES** -- We bought this Honda Civic because of the great gas mileage...

- **WHAT A GREAT COMMUTER CAR! - 36 M-P-G** -- I have saved so much money on gas since buying this...

Your job is now simple: copy and paste your Craigslist vehicle description into the AutoTrader **Online Ad Contents** section. When a buyer finds your car on their search results page, only 20 to 30 words of the vehicle description will be visible. To read the full description, they need to click on your listing.

So your Vehicle Description must include the most important content in those first 20 to 30 words. You may have to shorten your headline if you want part of the opening sentence included.

There are two other changes you need to make to your Craigslist description.

- There is no way to add attention-grabbing niceties like **bold,** *italics,* or underline. Nor can you separate the paragraphs, so your Craigslist ad will run into one long, difficult-to-read paragraph on AutoTrader.

   To compensate: (a) TRY CAPITALIZING THE FIRST FEW WORDS of the first sentence of the second paragraph. Or, (b) capitalize KEY WORDS to help the reader DISCRIMINATE THE CONTENT and make it easier to read.

   Go easy on using ALL CAPS:

   - **IF YOU USE TOO MANY, YOUR BUYER WILL FEEL LIKE YOU'RE YELLING AT THEM.** (Sorry, but an example is the best way to get the message across.)

- Because AutoTrader automatically adds so much detail to the full ad, you don't need to include **Itemized Vehicle Details** at the end of the vehicle description. Do include the following benefits, if they apply. These form part of the Itemized Vehicle Details from your Craigslist ad:

   - Vehicle History Report available

   - More pictures available

   - Walk-Around Video available

   - Clear title

Make sure the last sentence of your ad includes your contact information. At the bottom of the **Ad Detail** page, complete the **Contact Information** section. Click **Next** and you're done with this page.

Photo Upload

- The first picture to upload is your **Primary Exterior Photo**. This is the *Money Shot* (see Chapter 9). It is used for the large image on the **Vehicle Details** page and for the Thumbnail Photo on the **Search Results** page. It is taken from a 45-degree angle of the driver's front side.

- The maximum picture size you can upload is 150k. In Chapter 9 I explain how to resize your photos to fit within this limit.

- Use the maximum number of pictures your package allows.

- When finished click **Next**.

Ad Review

- There is an **Edit** link available for each section. This allows you to go back and make changes.

- Near the bottom you'll find the **Online Search Results Listing**. Click **Enlarge** on the right side. Here you can determine if the **Search Results Vehicle Description** is maximized for effect. Is the whole Headline included, along with enough of the personalized description to make sense AND interest the reader? If not, click **Edit** and make changes.

- Help is never far away. You can contact a real person via live chat by clicking **Questions? Click for Live Help**.

- When finished, click **Next**.

Ad Enhancements

- Everything offered here is useful, but *you* need to determine what is cost effective for your ad. Balance the added costs with your budget considerations.

- As a dealer, the most valuable enhancements are the **Premium Listing** and **Featured Spotlight**. Both determine how quickly, and how often, your ad will be read.

  This is particularly important when your listing has a lot of competition. That's why I had you run a search for comparable vehicles. It is crucial to get your ad as close to the top as possible, unless there are only a few on the **Search Results** page.

  When in doubt, put your money into enhancements that increase your visibility.

- When finished, click **Next**.

Checkout

- Once you have completed this section, click **Submit Order.** Your transaction is complete.

Changing Your Ad

You can change or update your ad at anytime. Simply go to www.autotrader.com. Click **Sell Your Car** in the upper bar. On the left side of the next page look for **Already Have An Ad?** Below it click **Edit or renew your ad.**

Stay Current

To stay at the top, premium websites have to
continually adjust to the fast moving currents.

The multi-billion dollars vehicle resale market is a shark tank.
The constant change means that the ad packages
I describe through this chapter may have
changed slightly by the time you read this.

Stay current. I keep an up-to-the-minute comparison
of AutoTrader and Cars.com on my website at
www.BayAreaCarGuy.com/premiumsites.

Part 2 — Creating Your Ad on Cars.com

Cars.com also provides a great service, has some useful tools, and is easy to use. Go to www.cars.com. Look for **Sell Your Car** in a box near the top, right side of the home page. After entering your ZIP, click **Sell My Car Now.**

Pricing Options

You are presented with a choice of Basic ($15),
Enhanced ($40), or Premium ($55) packages.

These prices are comparable with AutoTrader.com,
except that, as of this writing, Cars.com does not offer
a free trial package, something AutoTrader added recently.

Knowing how competitive this marketplace is, I expect Cars.com to catch-up soon. Compare the most current differences between AutoTrader and Cars.com at www.BayAreaCarGuy.com/premiumsites.

The major differences of the three plans are the duration of the listing and the number of pictures you can post. Your credit card won't be processed until the very end, so play around with the different packages until you get what you want, at a price you can afford.

AutoTrader offers pricey options to get your ad placed near the top. Cars.com is more user-oriented in how search results are listed. A pull-down menu on its search results page sorts results based on the buyer's preferences, not by who paid the most to be near the top.

This sort feature has two implications for the seller:

1. Fewer pricey options resulting in:

   – potentially lower costs

   – less opportunity to manipulate your placement in search results.

2. A better chance of being found by buyers based on what actually matters to them:

   – price

   – mileage

   – model year

   – engine

   – distance to travel

Once you choose your plan, you're taken to the **Build Your Ad** page. Look carefully at your car to confirm its actual features, or a do a Google search of your make, model, and year to determine them.

> *Completing this page as completely and accurately*
> *as possible can make the difference between*
> *selling your car or not—or selling for its full value.*

In the **Vehicle Type** section (at the top of the page), there's a handy **Price Your Car Right** tool which allows you to confirm the price you have already established. It appears after you've completed selections from the drop down menus. Refer back to Chapter 3 if you still have questions about pricing your vehicle.

Here's a Chance to Check Out the Competition

To show you an example, I created a **Build Your Ad** page with information on my 2006 Honda Civic in the **Vehicle Type** section. The **Price Your Car Right** tool let me know how the competition stacked up.

Below the current pricing figures it gave me this option: **View 29 similar vehicles for sale on Cars.com.** Clicking on **View 29** presented a search page for Honda Civics within a 10 miles radius.

What I discovered bodes well for using the
New Rules described in HELP! I Gotta Sell My Car NOW!

Twelve of the 29 Honda Civics did not have a picture. Too bad for the folks who didn't know that they were losing buyers.

There were 28 dealer listings and just one private seller. Cars.com initially levels the playing field for both dealers and private sellers by not allowing personalized content in search results. Your vehicle will be judged by these basic criteria:

- year

- make

- model

- mileage

- price

- one picture

With Cars.com the buyer has the option of sorting results based on her preference. Results can be listed with the lowest priced vehicles first, or any of the following:

- newest or oldest first

- by mileage

- body style

- engine size

- distance to you

If you pass muster here and a buyer clicks on your listing, they will see the rest of your ad where you have personalized the content to set yourself apart.

Why is it important to personalize your ad? Go back to the search results. Click on dealer ads to see their **Selling Points** and **Condition** details. Some dealers ignore how much they are paying for each listing:

- They don't add any information under Selling Points or Condition so these sections don't even show up in their listing.

- Some use VIN explosions to describe their vehicle.

- Still others include a generalized sales pitch for their dealership, instead of including useful information about the car itself. They will even copy and paste a song and dance on why you should contact their Internet Department.

  Buyers don't waste time with these shilly-shallies because there is nothing useful. Dealers are training buyers to skip their ads.

Onward

Continue to work your way down the page by completing the **Vehicle Information** section and the first part of the **Vehicle Description** section.

Personalizing Your Ad

Cars.com inserts basic information about your car at the top of your listing—year, make, model, mileage, price, and other basic information—then provides more details in the **Features** section.

What Buyers Want

The casual buyer surfing search results won't pay much attention to the detailed Features found at the top of your ad.

They're familiar with the make and model.

What they want is more information about your specific car. Their gaze will drop down to the Selling Points and Condition sections—the two opportunities you have to personalize your listing.

Copy your Craigslist ad into the **Additional Selling Points** area of the **Vehicle Description** section. You are limited to 1,000 characters here, and again in the Condition section.

The system will tell you if you run over your allotment. Don't worry about duplicating features listed in Features. Repetition of your car's main selling points is useful.

Your Craigslist ad should have an ALL CAPS headline, followed by personalized notes. See examples earlier in this chapter. Make sure the last sentence of your ad includes your contact information. There are two changes you need to make to your Craigslist descriptions:

- There is no way to add attention-grabbing niceties like **bold**, *italics* or <u>underline</u>. Nor can you separate the paragraphs, so your Craigslist ad will run into one long, difficult-to-read paragraph on Cars.com.

  To compensate: (a) CAPITALIZE THE FIRST FEW WORDS of the second paragraph. (b) capitalize KEY WORDS to help the reader discriminate the CONTENT and make it EASIER to read.

  Go easy on using ALL CAPS:

  - **OR YOUR BUYER WILL FEEL LIKE YOU'RE YELLING AT THEM.** (See how that feels?)

- Do not include the Itemized Vehicle Details, as Cars.com inserts most of this information automatically.

  Do include the following benefits, if they apply. These form part of the Itemized Vehicle Details from your Craigslist ad:

  - Vehicle History Report available

  - More pictures available

  - Walk-Around Video available

  - Clear title

Complete the Condition section with your personalized information in one of two ways:

- Move the condition information out of Additional Selling Points section and into the Condition section.

- Write about the condition of your car, and don't worry about duplicating information.

Which one you choose is a judgment call based on how the ad reads. If the bulk of the Selling Points is about your car's condition, you should write two distinct pieces. Otherwise, some duplication is fine. In either case, CAPITALIZE as suggested above.

When you have completed inputting all information on this page, click **Next: Add Photo(s) or I'll add my photos later.** Because pictures are so important in creating an effective ad, include your photo(s) now if you have them.

Photo Upload

The first picture to upload is your Primary Exterior Photo, the Money Shot (see Chapter 9). Cars.com places a large image on the **Vehicle Details** page and a **Thumbnail Photo** on the **Search Results** page.

Cars.com should automatically resize your photos
to match their system requirements.
If you prefer to resize them ahead of time,
I explain how to in Chapter 9.

Use the maximum number of pictures your package allows.

When finished, click **Next: Review Ad**. You can also **Modify Photo, Edit Information,** or at the bottom, **Preview Ad**.

Help

Help is just a phone call away: 1-888-780-1286. However, unlike the superb availability of Help on the AutoTrader site, Cars.com Help is only available 9am to 5pm CST Monday through Friday. If you want to contact them after those hours or by email, use the email contact form that can be found on most pages.

Checkout

Once you have reviewed all information, click **Next: Check Out,** or the link below that for PayPal.

Changing Your Ad

You can change or update your ad at any time. Simply go to www.cars.com. In the Sell Your Car box on the upper-right side of the home page, click **Sign In to Edit or Renew Your Ad**. Once you have signed in, you'll find your existing ad under **Manage Your Ads**. Click on it to make changes.

Good luck! And for goodness sakes, try to have fun with the process.

Need HELP?

I offer two levels of support to private sellers who feel they could use a little help with their online ad. The **Quick Consult** and **Write My Ad** are available on my **Need Help?** page at BayAreaCarGuy.com. Car dealers can look on the **Dealers** page for support available to them.

8

Matching Your *Words* to the Buyer's *Needs:*

The Buying Criteria that Best Describe Your Vehicle

One of the first things that a car salesperson finds out from a prospective buyer is *why* they are looking for a new vehicle. This "needs assessment" helps match the person to an appropriate vehicle. It also provides information to help close the deal later on.

For example, if your customer is a 25-year old who is looking for a powerful 2-seater sports car, there's no need to stress how economical a car it is. He cares about speed, specs, and performance. His primary *buying criterion* is performance.

Secondary Buying Criterion

There is usually a secondary buying criterion worth emphasizing. In the case of a sports car, it's likely to be comfort—like leather seats and a quality sound system.

On the other hand, a family with three small children looking for a minivan is primarily concerned with safety. You don't have to promote horsepower or the time to go from 0 to 60 mph.

Instead, direct our attention to the side curtain air bags, electronic stability control, ABS brakes, TETHER child seat system, and near-perfect crash test rating.

The secondary buying criteria for family minivans are usually economy or convenience. Thus, focus on fuel economy and low cost, OR the fact that the van has power sliding side doors and a rear DVD entertainment center.

Emotions Rule

Buying a new or used vehicle is often an emotional experience. As buyers get caught up in car ads—and TV or online hype—thinking of buying a vehicle gets exciting, something to look forward to.

However, the fantasies portrayed by the car manufacturers can work against you:

A Costly Example

As an Internet Manager, I worked with one family whose circumstances cried out for an inexpensive, economical sedan. Despite my effort to steer them toward what would serve their actual needs, they drove home in a gas-guzzling SUV that was sure to suck the air out of their budget. Try as you might, you can't always protect people from themselves.

This is why professionals want to know why you need another vehicle. If they can discover what's essential behind a purchase, they can use the information to the advantage of both the customer and the dealer:

- They can help the customer find a vehicle that actually fills a need and serves their purpose.

- It provides the dealer with specific information to please their customer and close a deal, so they can move another car off their lot.

Good News

The process is simpler for the private seller. A dealer assesses their customer to find the best vehicle out of many on the lot. As a private seller, you simply have to determine which buying criteria best describes your vehicle, then build your online ad using the key words and phrases I provide.

Unlike a dealer, you aren't matching a car to the customer's buying criteria. Instead, you are announcing to the world (or at least your corner of the world) the buying criteria that match your vehicle, and so buyers can find you.

If the words you use in your posting accurately reflect **what** the buyer is looking for—and more importantly, **why** the buyer is looking for a particular model—you just went to the top of their short list of cars to look at.

The Top Ten Key Words List

The Top Ten Key Words list is taken from all criteria. These are the features that matter most to most buyers. Emphasize these in your Posting Title and Posting Description.

I developed this list as a result of posting hundreds of ads online each month. If it's on this list, it's because buyers respond to them. These are the features that buyers go out of their way to look for. *If you've got it, flaunt it!*

The Top Ten Key Words

1. 1-Owner

2. Leather

3. Navigation

4. Moon Roof

5. DVD Entertainment Center

6. Third Row Seat

7. Heated Seats

8. Special Drivetrain:

    – 4x4

    – AWD

9. Special wheels:

    – Alloy Wheels

    – Chrome Wheels

    – Custom Wheels

    – Premium Wheels

10. Comes with warranty:

    – Extended Warranty

    – Remaining Factory Warranty

Buying Criteria

After checking the Top Ten Key Words list, determine which Buying Criteria apply to your vehicle. I have simplified the buying criteria categories that are used by most dealers to just four, plus an extra catchall General category. They are:

Economy

Emphasize low initial cost and low operating expenses.

- If you are selling an economy car that has **extra features**, emphasize those too.

    - For example, if your 2008 Chevy Aveo has power windows and locks, be sure to give those priority in your post.

- Listing the **exact gas mileage** for vehicles is important here. www.fueleconomy.gov shows EPA fuel economy rating for any vehicle.

    - The EPA changed the way it calculates EPA rating beginning with 2008 models. Most ratings went down. For 2007 and earlier models, use the "Official EPA MPG" (it's higher than the "Estimated New MPG").

Safety

This category is often referred to as the "family" category. However, "safety" can apply to anyone. For example, if a parent is buying their daughter her first car, safety is likely the primary concern. Or if your buyer was in a recent car accident, chances are they are also quite concerned about safety issues.

- Search Google for the year, make, and model of your car to find a detailed listing of its **original equipment**.

    - This usually includes safety equipment, such as the number of air bags, ABS brakes, etc. It's useful information to highlight in your post.

- Curious about the government **crash test rating** for your vehicle? Include a rating that is high in your post. Find it at www.safercar.gov.

Convenience/Comfort

This category is not limited to luxury cars. "Convenience" features are available on the high-end trim lines of even the least expensive economy models.

- Don't be afraid to **list every imaginable feature**. However, begin with the extra features and most expensive accessories for your particular make and model.

- For example, if you paid extra for a moon roof and premium wheels, include those first.

Performance
It's about speed and power.

Go crazy detailing the **specifications and extra features** on your vehicle.

Include your personal experience with your vehicle, including *why* you bought a car with these features, *what* your favorite features are, and *how much* you enjoy them.

General
Look here no matter which other categories are used. Include the features that apply to your vehicle.

Keep In Mind

Most vehicles have a primary category,
with one or more secondary ones.

Emphasize the primary features first.

Check the **Top Ten Key Words list** AND the **General category**,
no matter which others you use.

Buying Criteria Categories

General
- 1-owner
- Low Miles
- Ultra Low Miles
- Alloy Wheels w/Wheel Locks
- 18-inch Chrome Wheels
- Front Brakes 75% – Rear 85%
- 85% Tire Tread Life Remaining
- Running Boards
- Fog Lights
- Tow Package
- Roof rack
- Roof Rack w/Snow Board Attachment
- Cargo Cover

- Cargo Tray Cover
- FlexFuel
- Extended Warranty
- Balance of the Factory Warranty
- Balance of the Manufacturer's Warranty
- Purchased as a Certified vehicle
- Purchased as a Certified Honda Used Car
- Clean CARFAX Report
- 4-wheel Drive
- 2-wheel Drive
- All Wheel Drive
- AWD
- Sedan
- Coupe
- Manual Transmission
- Auto Transmission
- 2.0L L4
- 3.0L V6
- Security System
- Rugged Interior
- Fully Maintained
- Regular Service

Economy

- 36 M-P-G
- 29 mpg/city
- 32 mpg/hwy
- Overall rating of 31 M-P-G
- Gas Saver
- Affordable
- Economical
- Great Gas Mileage

Safety

- ABS Brakes
- 4-Wheel Disc Brakes
- Side Curtain Air Bags
- 4 Air Bags
- 6 Air Bags
- Traction Control
- Vehicle Stability Assist (VSA)
- Electronic Stability Assist

Convenience/Comfort
- Navigation
- GPS
- Bluetooth
- Hands-free
- Power Driver's Seat
- 8-way Power Driver's Seat
- Power Front Seats
- Homelink
- Keyless Entry
- Power Sliding Doors (minivan)
- Power Side Vent Windows
- Power Windows
- Power Windows – Locks – Side-mirrors
- Cruise Control
- Tilt Wheel
- Air – Cruise – Tilt
- Air Conditioning
- Climate Control
- Dual Climate Control
- Rear Climate Control
- Tinted Windows
- Privacy Windows
- Limo Tint (darkest tint available)
- AM-FM Radio
- AM-FM-CD Player
- Heated Seats
- Heated Front Seats
- Leather-wrapped Steering Wheel
- Audio controls on the steering wheel
- Premium Sound
- Premium Sound w/7 speakers & sub-woofer
- Thunderous Sound System
- Satellite Radio
- XM Satellite Radio w/170 digital-quality channels
- 6-CD Changer
- CD + Cassette Player
- D-V-D
- DVD w/2 wireless headsets
- iPod-MP3 Jack w/USB Connection
- Aux Jack
- 2 power outlets by the driver so you can charge two cell phones at once

- Leather
- Soft, tan leather seats
- Moon Roof
- Performance
- 197 HP
- 3.0L V6
- 5.7L V8 HEMI
- V8 POWER
- Black-on-black
- Powerful
- Sporty
- Manual
- 6-speed Manual
- Tiptronic Shifter
- Hurst Shifter
- Bling-Bling
- Bling Wheels
- 22-inch Blings
- Alloy Wheels
- Chrome Wheels
- Premium Wheels
- Rear Spoiler
- Lip Spoiler
- Wing Spoiler

9

Photos — Photos — Photos

Taking Effective Pictures that SELL Your Vehicle

The purpose of posting effective pictures—and lots of them—is to get prospective buyers so enthused about your vehicle that they immediately pick up the phone.

Successful car dealers know that the more photos they use, the better the chance of a vehicle selling. Learn from the pros: use the maximum number of pictures allowed on each website— or in the case of premium websites, the most expensive package you can afford.

Host Photos Online

You can overcome website limitations by having extra pictures available to email, or by uploading them to websites that specialize in hosting photos. Check the **Tools** page at www.BayAreaCarGuy.com/tools for a list of sites to use.

Another advantage of having lots of pictures of your vehicle is that it builds your buyer's trust that you are a competent seller who is accurately representing your car. Using sloppy pictures is a picture of a sloppy *you*. Are you hiding something? Or just incompetent? *Ouch!* That sounds harsh. But is this the first impression you really want to give?

Plenty of good pictures can initially mean fewer questions for you to deal with. Later, that trust will support you during the inherent stress of price negotiations and paperwork.

Preparation

- **Cheap is good** – For private sellers (not dealers), the least expensive, most basic digital camera available today takes acceptable pictures. What is important is a camera that you can hold at odd angles while keeping subject matter centered. Ultra-close-ups require a Macro setting, but don't buy a new camera for just that.

If you want an excellent wide angle camera (dealers, this applies to you) that's not too expensive, see the **Tools** page on my website at www.BayAreaCarGuy.com/tools. Chad Manz, a leading authority on automotive online marketing, especially photos, shares the most up-to-date technology recommendations and I pass them on to you.

- **Use a pleasant background** – Can you park your car near trees or water for the picture shoot? Is there a hill overlooking a broad expanse nearby? Avoid parking against a wall, or in any tight, restrictive, or dark space.

If your options are limited, try a neutral background like an empty corner of a parking lot at a shopping center.

- **Take bright daylight pictures** – You don't want buyers thinking you have something to hide. Dim light makes it difficult to see details.

- **Avoid shadows or reflections** – This applies to shadows of yourself, trees or buildings, though you can't always avoid them. Try moving the vehicle—reversing or rotating its position, or finishing later when the sun has shifted. (*Avoid shots like this one: photographer shadow in bottom left corner*).

- **Don't get fancy** – Simple is better. Don't use artistic angles that jar the reader's attention. This includes taking shots from above looking down, or from below looking up at the car. (*Avoid shots like this one: looking up at car.*)

Or too far away. (*Avoid shots like this one: too much space around the car.*)

Simple, eye-level pictures that fill the frame are preferred. The exception is taking close ups of the car's features, such as the wheels, 4x4 or other badging, moon roof, etc.

- **Interior shots** – Chad Manz recommends parking the car in the shade to avoid background glare and light variations of direct sunlight for interior photos. You'll probably use your flash for these. *(Avoid shots like this one: bright sunlight mixed with dark shadow.)*

- **More examples** – If you are selling an SUV, truck, sports car, or simply want to see more examples of online pictures, go to my website at www.BayAreaCarGuy.com/photos. More photo layouts and other resources are also available there.

Taking Photos

There are a number of standard photos that every seller should email prospective buyers or upload to a website like PhotoBucket. These are the most important ones:

Primary exterior photo. Always begin here: the *front driver's side corner view.* This is the *money shot.* It's the first photo to post. It provides the best detail of the front and side. It's a 45-degree angle looking at the front bumper on the driver's side.

Before taking the picture, turn the steering wheel all the way to the right so the front wheel is exposed.

Front exterior

Passenger's side front corner exterior

Passenger's side rear corner exterior

Rear exterior

Driver's side rear corner exterior

Driver's side exterior

Driver's side interior view

Driver's center view

Steering wheel and gauge cluster

Center console

Center console close up

Lower center console close up

Passenger's side view

 **Front seats driver's view**

 **Rear seats front view**

 **Rear seats side view**

 **Driver's door**

 **Passenger's door**

 **Trunk**

Engine bay

Tire tread

Wheel (alloy, chrome, or wheel covers)

Additional Photos

Hatchback with folding rear seats? You find these features on many SUV and crossover vehicles. Include the following series of photos.

- Take shots from the rear with the hatchback up, looking in—with the seats and cargo cover up, if one is installed.

- If there are three rows of seating, take pictures with all the seats up, then with the last row down, and finally with both rear rows down. You can even add a picture with part of one row up and the rest down, like this one.

- Your final photo in this series has all seats down to show the actual space available.

Vehicle Identification Number (VIN). This can add credibility AND provide a verified VIN so buyers can obtain their own vehicle history reports. Use the macro setting on your camera to get everything focused. Look under the hood or inside the driver's door for the VIN plate.

Other Major Selling Features

Check the Top Ten Key Word list and major Buying Criteria items. If your vehicle has them, include a picture to *sell* the feature. Here are some ideas:

Tow package? Kneel down at a slight side angle.

4-wheel drive? Picture the 4x4 emblem or badging on the side or rear of the vehicle.

Exterior badging? V6? V8? XLE model? If it's noteworthy, post a picture.

Running boards? Shoot from a 45-degree angle, either from the front or rear, looking down from eye level.

Moon roof? Getting the angle correct can be difficult. See the example.

DVD entertainment section? Fully open the screen and shoot from the rear seat looking forward. Avoid a lot of light coming through the windshield by parking in a shaded area. If there are headsets, take a separate picture *with* the owner's manual sitting on the rear seat.

Navigation? Have the display on and pull back slightly to show buttons, joystick, and other controls.

Manuals and keys? Having all of the owner's manuals, keys, and remotes is important to some buyers. It can cost up to $200 to replace each programmable key. Owner's manuals can also be expensive. So if you have them, flaunt them. Set the manuals and keys in an open space and take a picture of them together. See the example.

Tires good? Show the tread life with a close-up, along with a wider shot shown earlier in this chapter.

Odometer reading. If your mileage is lower than comparable vehicles on the market, a picture of the odometer is a great selling feature. To get the picture focused correctly, set the camera to its Macro setting. Check your camera's user guide for instructions. If you are taking extra pictures to email or upload, include the odometer shot no matter what the mileage.

Rag top? If you are selling a convertible, take all the exterior pictures with the top up, then repeat the series with the top down.

Photo Layout

The first picture you upload is always the Primary exterior photo. This is your first and best picture. Following are suggested photo layouts for the different size photo packages available. Modify what you post to show the best selling features of your vehicle, and to limit what is not ideal.

For example, if the engine bay under the hood is dirty and grimy because you haven't gotten around to cleaning it yet, or if the trunk is filled with junk because you didn't have time to remove it, don't include these shots. However, if you have dents, scratches, or other defects that you feel the buyer should know about, do include them.

The following photo layouts are suggestions. Alter their content and order based on the best selling features of your vehicle. But remember to upload your Primary exterior photo first, every time. **Photo layout examples with pictures are available at www.BayAreaCarGuy.com/photos.**

1-Photo Layout (AutoTrader & Cars.com)

- Primary exterior

3-Photo Layout (AutoTrader & Cars.com)

- Primary exterior
- Passenger's side rear corner exterior
- Driver's side interior view

4-Photo Layout (Craigslist, Oodle, & Backpage)

- Primary exterior
- Passenger's side rear corner exterior
- Driver's side interior view
- Best feature—such as premium wheels, odometer, cargo bay with seats down, clean engine bay, etc.

8-Photo Layout (Kijiji)

- Primary exterior
- Passenger's side rear corner exterior
- Driver's side interior view
- Steering wheel and gauge cluster
- Center console
- Rear seat side view
- Best feature—such as premium wheels, odometer, cargo bay with seats down, clean engine bay, etc.
- Trunk—or for an SUV, show the cargo bay with seats down

9-Photo Layout (AutoTrader)

- Primary exterior
- Passenger's side rear corner exterior
- Driver's side interior view
- Steering wheel and gauge cluster
- Center console
- Rear seat side view
- Best feature—such as premium wheels, odometer, cargo bay with seats down, clean engine bay, etc.
- Second best feature—such as premium wheels, odometer, cargo bay with seats down, clean engine bay, etc.
- Trunk—or for an SUV, show the cargo bay with seats down

12-Photo Layout (Cars.com)

- Primary exterior
- Driver's side rear corner exterior
- Passenger's side rear corner exterior
- Passenger's side front corner exterior

- Driver's side interior view
- Passenger's side view
- Steering wheel and gauge cluster
- Center console
- Rear seat side view
- Best feature—such as premium wheels, odometer, cargo bay with seats down, clean engine bay, etc.
- Second best feature—such as premium wheels, odometer, cargo bay with seats down, clean engine bay, etc.
- Trunk—or for an SUV, show the cargo bay with seats down

18-Photo Layout (AutoTrader)

- Primary exterior
- Front exterior
- Passenger's side front corner exterior
- Passenger's side rear corner exterior
- Rear exterior
- Driver's side rear corner exterior
- Driver's side exterior
- Driver's side interior view
- Passenger's side view
- Steering wheel and gauge cluster
- Center console
- Rear seat front view
- Rear seat side view
- Best feature—such as premium wheels, odometer, cargo bay with seats down, clean engine bay, etc.
- Second best feature—such as premium wheels, odometer, cargo bay with seats down, clean engine bay, etc.
- Tire tread or wheel
- Engine bay
- Trunk—or for an SUV, show the cargo bay with seats down

Getting Photos Up Online

- **Use the maximum number of photos available on each website** – Craigslist allows you to use four photos, while Kijiji lets you post eight. The premium sites vary depending on which package you purchase. Use the maximum available, or the most you can afford.

- **Have more photos available** – I take a minimum of 30 pictures per car, and often take 60 or more for an SUV, luxury sedan, or sports car. Many buyers appreciate this amount of detail—it confirms you don't have anything to hide and it sets you apart from the crowd as someone they can trust. Have the extra pictures ready to email, or link to a website where you have posted them.

- **Need to resize?** Some websites limit the size of the pictures you can upload. Check the **Tools** page at www.BayAreaCarGuy.com/tools for websites that offer resizing.

A New Career?

Taking pictures for online car ads is
something you become better at with practice.

If you develop a talent for this, let your friends know.
Most people know someone who will be selling a vehicle.
A picture is worth a thousand words, and if folks hear that you
actually know what you're doing, your skills will be in demand.

Dealers across the country are also looking for someone
who can lift the burden of bad online photos from their shoulders.

Stay tuned for the BayAreaCarGuy's *Dealer Online Photo Guide*:
Your Opportunity to Lead the Industry in this Emerging Field.

Finally...

The photos you use for your online ad play a big part in the response you'll get from buyers, both positive and negative. Refer to the **Photos** page at www.BayAreaCarGuy.com/photos for examples of the best ways to present your vehicle online.

10 The Video Walk-Around

A Secret Weapon that Anyone Can Master

The video walk-around is the secret weapon that brought me serious customers when I was Internet Sales Manager. Remember my customer who drove eleven hours round trip to buy a car from me?

There were many reasons why he was willing to work with an unknown dealer so far away, but the clincher was the video walk-around of the car.

I shot the video just for him, beginning with "Hi Geoff," and used it to answer his specific concerns about the car. It was like continuing our phone conversations, except I was the only one talking. He could see the details he was concerned about: the dent in the bumper and a scratch on the driver's door.

Talk about a captive audience. How cool is that?

> *The video walk-around confirmed that*
> *everything I had said was true.*

Because he was driving so far, I even negotiated the price over the telephone. This is usually a no-no (read Chapter 11 to find out why), but I did it to dissolve his resistance to making the drive.

When he arrived, he simply checked the car's condition with a test drive, and I verified that he would get the price we had negotiated. He saw that everything was as he expected, so he signed the contract and gladly drove home in his new-to-him car.

The selling was done long before he arrived at the dealership. In my experience, it is rare for someone to make a long drive after viewing a video walk-around and NOT buy the vehicle.

Making the Sale

The video and our prior conversations made the sale. Buyers make
the trip to simply confirm the details and pick up the car.

Shifting into Reverse

Be prepared for the opposite experience, because the video walk-around helps sort buyers into two general categories:

- those who want to buy your car

- those who do NOT want to buy your car

I use the walk-around to help my buyers determine if this is the car for them, not to push the car on them. As a result, some buyers saw the video and crossed my car off their list. Great! He saved us both time and energy. Others saw the video and made the decision to see it in person. Also great! We made a deal. Be prepared for both responses. For both, it's worth making the video.

I also make a video walk-around for customers who live close by. People who are busy (which is most people) appreciated the service. Based on their reaction, I know that I am developing a relationship with them that no one else has:

*A relationship that not only puts my car in the running,
but propels it to the top of their short list.*

My car still has to win the race on its own merits of condition and price. But the video walk-around gives me a head start over all other sellers.

Getting Ready to Make the Video

- **Prep your car** – Clean it inside and out, and remove ALL personal items.

- **Find a location** – You need a lot of extra room immediately outside the car, and a certain amount of privacy. Choose a pleasant background, like the one you used for the photo shoot. One near trees or water, or on a hill overlooking a broad expanse is preferred. An empty parking lot at a shopping center actually works well for this. Avoid parking against a wall, or in tight, restrictive, or dark space.

- **Shoot in the daylight** – You don't want buyers thinking you have something to hide. Dim light makes it difficult to see the detail of your vehicle.

- **Avoid windy days** – You don't want wind to drown out your voice. The same can hold true for a surfside setting.

- **Avoid shadows or reflections** – This applies to shadows of you, trees or buildings. If you can't avoid your shadow, pick a place where you're not walking in and out of direct sunlight. The car itself should be fully in the sun or the shade—not both.

- **Equipment** – You can use a high-end video camera or a simple point and shoot digital camera with video and audio function. People are surprised that I use a small, pocket-size digital camera for all my videos. I only paid extra for a large memory card so I can do as many takes as I want. Check your owner's manual on how the video function works. Check the **Tools** page on my website at www.BayAreaCarGuy.com/tools for up-to-date recommendations on which cameras to use.

- **Don't get fancy** – Begin thinking simple—both for the script and the physical walk-around.

Two Script Options — General or Personal?

Are you creating a video for *anyone* who's interested in your car? Will you upload to the Internet so anybody can find it?

Or is it *personalized* to address specific concerns for a buyer you are already talking to? There are different considerations depending upon your intention:

- **General Video** – Begin by refreshing your memory. Refer back to the vehicle description in your online ad. What are your major selling points, features, *and the personal story behind your car?* What do you like most, and why? Why did you buy it, and why are you selling? Based on the Key Words and Buying Criteria, what features stand out? Why would someone be interested in THIS car?

  - Low miles?

  - Great condition?

  - Clean vehicle history report?

  - Powerful engine?

  - Great gas mileage?

  - Moon roof?

  - Premium wheels?

  Now that you have refreshed your memory about the positive features, what negative aspects of your car do you want the buyer to know?

If YOU were driving a few hours to see the car, what would YOU want to be told before making the trip?

— Scratches on the front and rear bumpers from parking in tight spaces? It's better to show them so the buyer isn't disappointed when she arrives.

— Dents on the driver's door from shopping carts gone wild? It happens.

— Alloy rims that hit the curb once too often, leaving permanent marks?

— Seats worn or stained? Well, it is a used car!

— Something not working properly? Honesty is the best policy.

- **Personalized Video** – For a specific buyer, personalize what you are describing. Did they have specific questions or concerns that you can address?

  — Did she question how large the dent on the driver's door is? Make this your first stop.

  — Did you gush over how perfect the exterior finish is? A picture is worth a thousand words.

  — The scratches on the bumpers? Better to know *now* if it's a deal breaker.

  — Does she know about the cigarette burn on the passenger's seat? It will help if she sees how small it is.

  — Does she love the premium wheels? Pump up her excitement.

  — If she isn't sure if the trunk is big enough, show her.

  It's like show-and-tell. Point out what matters, and address her by name.

Make your list of points now, because we're about to plot out the walk-around.

How long should your video be?

3 minutes is ideal.
Most will run 2 ½ to 3 ½ minutes.

It can be longer if you make it interesting
or are dealing with a specific list of concerns for a buyer.

Start at the Money Shot!

Always begin your video at the spot where you take the primary exterior photo. It's a 45-degree angle looking at the front bumper on the driver's side. It clearly shows both the front and driver's side. This is the best picture of your car for both a still shot and a video.

If the clean engine bay is a big selling feature, have the hood up. Otherwise leave it down. Have the trunk open if you plan to show it. Otherwise close it. The driver's door should be open, along with the passenger's side rear door.

Some people are simply too nervous to add their voice to their video. It's better to send a silent walk-around of the car than no video at all. However, adding audio increases the effectiveness. Whether you choose to use audio or not, shoot the video in the sequence described below.

A Picture is Worth a Thousand Words

Go to my **Video** page at BayAreaCarGuy.com/video
to see examples of what a video walk-around looks like.

I include one of the first videos I ever recorded,
of the Honda Civic SI Mugen Special Edition.
The video has over 70,000 hits and counting on YouTube.

The Walk-Around

You may want to skip ahead to read about the walk-around presentation in *Chapter 11 – Inquiries and Test Drives*. There I describe how to do an in person walk-around presentation before the test drive. Our task with the video walk-around is similar.

I teach the one-take, point-of-view (POV) video walk-around:

- **One-take** – I choose to shoot in one-take because viewers respond to the authenticity and raw reality of a one-take video walk-around. It shows that you don't have anything to hide—the good, the bad, and the ugly. I want my walk-arounds to be real in that way. It builds trust and develops a rapport with the buyer.

  If you know how to edit video, feel free to shoot in segments and edit them together.

- **Point-of-view (POV)** – The viewer sees the car through my eyes, rather than seeing me pointing to the car. I am never seen in the shot, except for my signature wave reflected in the car window. I also use the POV technique for practical reasons. I don't have to find someone to follow me with the camera.

Don't be limited by my methods. Once you have mastered my way for a video walk-around, feel free to experiment with different forms and techniques, both with yourself and others. Be creative and **have fun**.

How To — Start at the Beginning

- **The mechanics of using your camera** – For a regular digital camera, simply hold the camera close to your face so you can see what you are shooting, and talk into the camera so the microphone picks up your voice. Look at the LCD monitor (the small screen), if your camera has one, rather than through the view finder.

- **It takes a little practice** – Can you shoot and talk at the same time? Check the quality after each shoot. You are not vying for an Academy Award. You simply want an informative video that helps the buyer see the car and become comfortable with you. Don't worry about small mistakes or a little stumbling.

- **Greeting** – Begin by introducing yourself:

  – *Hi, this is James Johnson and I'm shooting a video of my 2006 Honda Civic EX.*

  – If you are recording the video for a specific person, begin with a personal greeting:

  Hi Bob, this is James Johnson with the video I promised of my 2006 Honda Civic EX.

- **Get your greeting out before you begin to move** – This is called establishing the shot. Let the viewer adjust to where you are before you move from the primary exterior shot.

  Once you've completed your greeting, begin to slowly move towards the front of the car, telling your story:

  – *I bought this Civic two years ago and don't drive it much, so the mileage is low, just 30-thousand miles. Let's checkout the front bumper and the scratches I mentioned on my online ad.*

- **More mechanics of shooting.**

  – You not only should move slowly, but don't swing the camera from side to side or up and down. Home videos tend to make viewers nauseous because of quick movements. Slow is better.

  – You also don't need to talk all the time. You can let the video convey what's relevant and enticing to a buyer—adding enough words to reveal what's personal.

How To — The Walk-Around

- **In the beginning** – You began the video at a 45-degree angle looking at the front bumper on the driver's side. After finishing the greeting and establishing the opening shot, slowly move to your left, telling your story in an easy and conversational manner.

- **Key stops** – It's crucial to SHOW the viewer what you want them to know about your car. Make a mental note of the stops you plan to make in your walk-around. Here are some common ones:

  – **Front bumper** – Scratches, scrapes, and dents, or the lack of them.

  – **Passenger's side** – Scratches and dents are common here, too. Is there a roof rack or other exterior accessory? Premium wheels? Show them in the order you reach them.

  – **Rear seat** – Have the rear door open on the passenger's side. This allows you to simply lean into the door opening with your head and camera as you describe what the viewer is seeing. When done, lean back out and continue toward the back of the car. If necessary, slip into the seat to show features such as a rear DVD entertainment system and climate controls.

- **Rear bumper** – More scratches or dents?

- **Badging** – Is there a V6 or V8 emblem on the side or rear of the vehicle? How about a 4x4 or AWD emblem? Is the manufacturer's model descriptor there, such as EXL, XLE or SC 400? Try to include badging in your walk-around.

- **Trunk** – If you plan on showing the trunk, have it open.

- **Driver's side** – More scratches or dents?

- **Driver's seat** – Your chance to slip in and sell the interior features, or describe what may be damaged.

- **Tire tread** – Want to show how new the tires are? Have the driver's side front wheel turned to the left, pointing away from the vehicle. After getting out of the driver's seat, kneel for a close up of the tread before stepping back to close the video. You can also shoot the wheel cover or premium rims here.

• **Transitions are important** – Do you need to kneel to get a close up of a dent or scratch? Let the viewer know what you are doing:

  – *I'm kneeling to get a better look at the scratch on the passenger's door that I told you about over the phone.*

  – *I know you are interested in the premium wheels. Give me a moment while I get low enough to give you a close up of what they're like.*

  – *I left the trunk open so I could show you how big it is. I know one of your concerns is trunk space, and as you can see this one is very roomy.*

• **The most important transition is moving from outside the car into the driver's seat** – As you move around the car you'll need to transition into the driver's seat (and/or the rear seat). Have the driver's door open and tell your viewer:

  – One of the best features of this Honda Civic is the factory navigation. Let me slip into the driver's seat so I can show you firsthand how big the screen is…

  – I want to show you how small the cigarette burn is on the passenger's seat. Give me a moment while I slip inside…

- **Transitioning out of the driver's seat** – Tell your viewer again. It can be short and simple:

  - *Give me a moment while I step out...*

  - *I want to show you the scratches on the back bumper. Hold on while I get out...*

- **Closing** – Finish where it all began. Move back to the Money Shot, a 45-degree angle looking at the front bumper on the driver's side.

  Keep the camera steady while closing your video. Don't worry about staying on a stationary shot for too long: you want the viewer to have a clear picture of what they hope to buy. And you want to give them time to write down your contact information.

  These final moments are your chance to review the best selling features and set the tone for how the buyer will think of you and your car in her deliberation process.

  Finish with your name and telephone number or email address. You never know who will see the video. If they are interested, they need to know how to reach you. If you are technically savvy, you can insert a caption onto the video displaying your contact information.

  Sample closes:

  - *Thanks for watching my video of this low mileage, 2006 Honda Civic. As you can see, it's in near-perfect condition. This is James Johnson. Call me at 510-648-0000 if you have questions. Bye for now.*

  - *I hope I have answered all your questions, Bob. If not, give me a call at 510-648-0000 and we can talk more about my 2006 Honda Civic. This is James Johnson. Bye for now.*

Remember that the purpose of the walk-around is to let buyers learn about both the car AND you. Don't try for perfection, and don't be afraid to let your personality loose.

Above all, have fun. Excitement and fun are contagious. There is no better way to sell your vehicle than communicating how excited you are about your car—and why.

Best Practices

The best way to learn how to record a video walk-around is:

Watch a sampling of video walk-arounds on the **Video** page
of my website at www.BayAreaCarGuy.com/video.

Then practice.
Watch the results.
Try again until satisfied.

Upload Your Video

It's time to upload your video to the Internet so you can send interested buyers a link to view it. There are many video hosting sites available. I use the most popular: YouTube.com.

YouTube not only allows prospective buyers to see your video through the link you send them, but it can be found by millions of people searching YouTube daily. This is your chance to shine:

- Go to www.YouTube.com.

- Click **Create Account** on the upper-right of the home page. Follow instructions.

- Once you have an account, click **Upload** on the upper-right of the home page.

- **AutoShare Options** on the next page give the choice to set up an auto post for FaceBook and Twitter. Your video will be automatically uploaded to each site.

  This is a great idea if you are already on FaceBook and Twitter. The more ways you can get your video in front of anyone—friends or strangers—the better. Once done, click **Upload Video**.

- While your video is uploading, complete the available **Video Information**:

  - **Title** – Name your video!

    o **For example:** *2006 Honda Civic Walk-Around by L. James Johnson.*

- **Description** – Tell what you are doing.

  - ○ **For example:** *My name is James Johnson and this is a video walk-around of my car that's for sale: 2006 Honda Civic EX...*

    Include your name, year, make, and model of your car, anything else useful, and your contact information.

- **Tags** – Tags are used by search engines to find your video. Complete this section if your video is for public viewing.

  List all the tag words that identify your video: year, make, model, features, buying criteria, your name, city, and state. (More is better.)

- **Category** – Choose **Autos and Vehicles**.

- **Privacy** – Choose **Share your video with the world** if it's a public video. Choose **Private** if not.

- Click **Save Changes**.

- Once the video is successfully uploaded, rest the cursor over your account name on the upper-right portion of the page. A drop down menu appears. Click **My Videos**.

- This give you access to your video where you can perform many functions:

  - Click **Edit** to update the Video Information

  - Click **Play** to get to the main control page for your video. (The video automatically starts when the new page loads. Hit **Pause** so we can take care of business.) In the box to the right, find the virtual keys to your video:

- **URL (web address)** – This is the link you will send to everyone interested in your car. Copy and paste the URL address into any email you send.

- **Embed** – This is code you insert into a website or blog to allow your video to play on the site itself. Technical issues abound: if you're not sure how to do this, get help.

How marvelous that your video allows all this networking. Be one of the few who takes advantage of these new opportunities:

- Send a link to your friends via email, instant messaging, or texting and ask them to pass it along to anyone who might be interested in your car. You finally get to have your own viral video!

- If you haven't used the **AutoShare Options,** be sure to manually upload the video on social networking sites such as FaceBook and Twitter.

  - Mention in your written intro that your car is for sale, along with one or two main selling points. Ask the reader to pass the video along to anyone who might be interested.

- Include the phrase, "Video Walk-Around Available!" in the ads you post on all classified websites.

11   Inquiries and Test Drives

How to Negotiate Like a Pro - And Be SAFE!

The purpose of creating an effective online ad for your car is to get buyers to contact you. Buyers tend to shop in spurts. They set aside time to call around for advertised vehicles, then work their way down a list of sellers, asking questions and making appointments to see and drive what looks promising.

Unless you are selling a rare or specialty car, you may be competing with 20 other similar postings.

If you don't answer their calls,
many buyers will cross you off their list.
You've just lost an opportunity
that you worked so hard to create.

Here are more cold, hard facts that the pros have learned:

- many buyers will *not* leave a voice message, but will simply call the next person on the list until they talk to a live person.

- even if they leave a message, most will have begun focusing on other vehicles and won't return your call.

The same is true with emails. The chance of selling your vehicle increases dramatically if you reply to an initial email inquiry within minutes. **Yes, that's minutes!** Email inquiries can have a very short shelf life. Waiting merely hours can kill your opportunity.

It's essential to respond to calls and emails as they come in. If you won't be available, arrange for a friend or family member to answer the phone and monitor your email account. *It's that important!*

Making Contact

I recommend providing as much contact information as you feel comfortable with and is appropriate for your personal circumstance. The more ways a prospective buyer can contact you, the better the chance of selling your vehicle.

Cell phone number and an email address are preferable. If you rely on land lines, include separate daytime and evening phone numbers. You're "on call" till your car is sold!

Consider setting up a disposable online email account. Using certain websites to post your ad, your regular email account may be vulnerable to unsolicited replies that have nothing to do with your vehicle. Yes, this is the dreaded s-p-a-m.

I recommend setting up a free online email account to use in all of your online ads. It's like creating a new identity, and it's okay to be inventive. Here are some examples:

- SellingMyMustang@gmail.com
- BuyMyCivic@hotmail.com
- ChevyForSale@yahoo.com
- FordsAreMyFriend@aol.com

You can choose your address to emphasize the main selling feature of your vehicle, so when someone types your email they are reminded of why they are contacting you. Point to the low mileage, immaculate condition, big chrome wheels, or the power of your truck like this:

- only6438miles@gmail.com
- NotAscratch@hotmail.com
- 22inchBlings@yahoo.com
- PowerfulChevyTruck@aol.com

Capitalize a few letters in the first half of your email address to make it readable with a simple glance. See which is easier to read:

- powerfulchevytruck@aol.com, or
- PowerfulChevyTruck@aol.com

Using this method allows you to be distinctive AND reinforces your major selling point. Best of all, it doesn't cost anything, and it can be fun. Don't forget the FUN.

Here's a list of some of the major free, online email accounts available:

- Gmail.com
- AOL.com
- Hotmail.com
- Yahoo.com

Handling Inquiries

The purpose of posting your ad is to get prospective buyers to contact you. From their contact you screen for credible buyers. In the phone or email response you'll provide additional information to filter out buyers who aren't really interested in your vehicle, and to satisfy those who are.

When you find that gem of a credible buyer, your task is to get the appointment, period.

If someone calls and wants to make an appointment:
STOP TALKING! Make the appointment.

Don't talk about price, paperwork, the weather, or anything else until you have an appointment. Getting chatty can inadvertently bring up reasons for the person NOT to see the car:

"Oh, I didn't know the tires weren't perfect. I won't bother coming over to see it after all." It may seem funny to you now, but you'll stop laughing the first time it happens.

Telephone is Preferred

Communicating with potential buyers is more effective on the telephone, though email is necessary at times:

- A real conversation allows the buyer to get to know you. This works in your favor because a real person with a real story tends to dissolve the natural fears we all have about dealing with strangers.

- An actual conversation can reveal a buyer's unformed questions and concerns. This is good because you can't resolve an issue you don't know about:

  - A buyer may have read about "Katrina cars" damaged in natural disasters that have flooded the used car market. When you tell them that your car has a clean vehicle history report, it opens the door to talking about what that means: no accidents, odometer issues, or natural disasters such as hurricanes.

    The buyer is relieved. Her unrecognized resistance might not have been addressed if you had been communicating with email.

- A real conversation allows you to ask some useful questions:

- Why do you need the car?

- What will you be using it for?

- Is it for you or a family member?

Based on the answers, you can address the buyer's situation. For example, if you know he is going to use the car for a long commute to work each day, you can reinforce the fact that it has low miles, heated seats, gets great gas mileage, and a high-end sound system.

After an initial email, ask if they would prefer to talk on the telephone in order for you to answer their questions more efficiently. But don't push.

Be Upfront and Honest

Chapter 4 clarifies the advantage that you have over dealers. You can personalize your ad in a way that most dealers can't, and you can avoid their negative image by being upfront and honest.

The NEW RULES of selling your car online include being transparent and not using gimmicks or tricks.

It's actually in your self-interest to be honest about your car. If someone is looking for a Chevy Impala that has a manual transmission, there is no point lying about the fact that your Impala has an automatic. Don't waste their time—or yours.

What about smaller, less obvious misdirections—or even lies—*that you may be able to get away with?*

- You decide *not* to tell a buyer about new scratches on the driver's door after she specifically told you that she was impressed with your convertible because your ad says the exterior is perfect.

  By remaining silent, you will likely sour the deal. Maybe you were hoping she wouldn't notice the scratches, but she did. Now she is disappointed, and you have lost credibility.

If she is still interested in your car, chances are the first words out of their mouth when you negotiate price will be:

I guess I could make you an offer, but I'm going to have to figure the cost of fixing the scratches on the driver's door.

Your omission just lost you $450. If you had included a picture of the scratch in your ad or mentioned it in the text or confirmed the scratches on the phone when she specifically asked about the paint job, there would be no unmet expectations.

You would have not only retained your credibility, you would have built trust and established a rapport with her, probably with little impact on the price. In this case, honesty would literally have put money in your pocket.

More often than not, being upfront and honest will work to your advantage. Most of us expect some imperfections in a used car. And we all respond favorably to honesty.

Setting Yourself Apart

Remember, being upfront and honest is how you, a private seller, can set yourself apart from the reputation of dealers and less-than-honest private sellers.

Dialing for Dollars

Most of the thousands of initial inquiries I've fielded from customers over the years included a question about price. When someone calls or emails for information, like is the car still available, they invariably ask one of the following:

- What's your best price?
- Is that the best you can do?
- Will you come down in price?

Everyone assumes you have built some "wiggle room" into your asking price. That's why my answer to the initial questions about price never varies:

> *Of course I'm flexible about the price.*
>
> *But there's not much point negotiating until you look at the car and give it a drive.*
>
> *If it's what you're looking for, I'm sure we can make a deal that works for you.*
>
> *Do you want to see it tonight or tomorrow?*

Learn from the pros: negotiating price by phone or email is a bad idea for the seller. The only exception to this rule is if the buyer has to travel a significant distance to see it.

If that's the case, or if you can't dissuade them from talking price, there are a few basic rules to follow. See *Negotiating 101* later in this chapter.

Showing Your Vehicle

As a dealer I made it a policy not to sell a car unless my customer drove it. Unless your buyer has a positive experience with the car, they can easily change their mind, especially if negotiations drag out or problems arise with the paperwork.

They not only want to make sure the seat is comfortable, but a test drive will let them know its general condition and if it drives and handles well.

A positive test drive experience is often enough incentive to push through any challenges that show up later.

Be Safe

Your first consideration in arranging a test drive with a stranger is your safety:

- Don't meet potential buyers at your home. Meet in a parking lot at a nearby shopping area or a fast food restaurant. One that is busy and filled with lots of people. Daytime is better.

- Bring a friend.

- Make sure friends or family know of your plans. Have them check in with you at a specific time following the test drive, if you don't call them first.

- Have your cell phone with you.

- Read the insurance section later in this chapter to make sure the buyer is covered by your insurance or theirs during the test drive.

- If you become suspicious of the buyer after meeting them in person, don't let them in the car, and have a pre-planned reason to leave immediately. More below.

The Walk-Around

Before the actual test drive is the time to *actively* sell your car. Pros call this the

Walk-Around:

- **Arrive early** – Before your potential buyer shows up. Clean up your car and remove ALL personal items. (It's difficult for the buyer to visualize the car as theirs if your CDs, papers, and fast food containers are strewn about.)

  Open the trunk and hood, as well as the driver's door if there is room where you parked. Move the driver's seat all the way back. Unlock all the doors.

  Have your keys in your pocket or purse. Don't take them out until later. NEVER give your keys to the buyer unless you are in the car with them.

- **Warm greeting** – When the buyer arrives, greet her warmly, smile and shake hands. Thank her for coming to see the car and say something like, "Let me take just a moment to show you a few things before you actually drive the car." Then walk to the front of your car.

- **Start at the front of the car** – If you didn't have time to open the hood, open it now. You might want to say something like:

  - I know very little about what is under the hood of cars these days. Here's the oil dip stick. There's the windshield washer fluid. Did you notice how clean the engine is? And, see, the belts and hoses are in good shape.

  Unless a buyer is mechanically minded, they will not linger at the engine. Time to move on.

- **Walk-around** – Close the hood and walk-around the passenger's side towards the rear. This is your opportunity to point out any positive features on the exterior including:

  - chrome, alloy or premium wheels, roof rack, moon roof, tow package, running boards, custom paint, etc.

  - the condition of the exterior, including the paint.

  - point out any scratches or dents (most likely on the front or rear bumpers). This should confirm previous information you gave over the telephone or in your pictures. The customer will be looking for scratches and dents; you gain credibility by pointing them out first.

- **Move to the rear** – Continue walking to the rear of the car. With the trunk open, show the spare tire and tools along with anything else of interest. Is the trunk big? Clean? Point out any rear seat release handles or levers in the trunk?

- **Walk-around** – Close the trunk and walk to the driver's side. You can open the rear door to show the back seat and any features in that area such as rear heating controls and rear DVD entertainment section. If appropriate, note the condition of the seats, the spaciousness, etc.

- **Move to the driver's door** – Open it, if it's not already open. Invite the buyer to try the seat. You know this car intimately, so tell the buyer how to adjust the seat. Leaning in slightly from the outside, show them how to move the seat forward or back, adjust the height, and secure the seat belt. If they are unfamiliar with this model, describe how the head light controls work, along with other dashboard features. Point out safety features such as side curtain air bags, traction control, and stability assist control.

- **Get inside** – Tell your buyer to stay where they are while you get in the passenger's seat. Now demonstrate the AM/FM/CD player, climate control, and the remaining features, including moon roof, side mirror controls, etc. You will need to put the key in the ignition to power some of these features.

- **Verify license and insurance** – This is a good time to verify their driver's license and insurance. Don't be afraid to ask to see the driver's license, and always check the expiration date to make sure it is still valid. See insurance information below.

- **Pass the keys** – Now bring out your keys and give them to the buyer, if you haven't done so already. NEVER give your keys to the buyer unless you are in the car with them.

Notice how you started at the front of the car and made a natural circle around to the driver's seat. It's a good idea to practice this with a friend a few times prior to meeting an actual buyer.

Ask them to give you feedback on whether your approach would be comfortable for them if they didn't know you. Keep practicing till you get comfortable with the process.

The Test Drive

Letting a stranger drive your car can feel odd. Here are some common sense suggestions to take into account:

- Accompany the buyer on the test drive. If you did the walk-around as described above, you are already in the passenger's seat and ready to go.

- Have a preplanned test drive route ready, one that includes a variety of traffic conditions, including local and highway roads, if possible. If the buyer knows the area, be flexible if they have their own route in mind. It's actually useful if they drive over familiar territory. However, always keep your safety in mind.

- Use your time on the test drive to point out features and benefits of the car.

- Be informative and answer any questions the buyer has. Being pleasant and helpful will allow the buyer to get to know you, and build a foundation for the negotiations that are looming on the horizon.

- Your safety is primary. If you become suspicious or unsure about a potential buyer:

    - Do NOT let them in your car.

    - Have a pre-planned reason to leave or simply say, "I'm sorry I wasted your time. Something has come up and I need leave right now. Again, I'm sorry. Bye." And leave. ***Your safety is more important than being polite.***

Insurance

Checking buyer's insurance will help you feel safe and protected.

Make sure *you* have full insurance coverage (see below). You also need to contact your insurance company to make sure that other people driving your car will be covered, as long as they have a valid driver's license (which is why you check) and your permission to drive the car.

> *If your insurance does not cover other people*
> *driving your car, you need to make sure*
> *that the buyer's insurance will provide*
> *full coverage while they are driving.*

Most Proof of Insurance cards don't provide the details of the coverage. This means that if your insurance will not cover the buyer, you need to ask them to bring proof of insurance AND details of their coverage (a copy of their actual policy) when you set the appointment.

Prior to letting them drive your car, confirm their full coverage, which includes collision, liability, and comprehensive.

If there is any doubt in your mind about insurance, and whether the buyer is covered or not, do not let them drive your car until you clarify the issue, either with a call to your insurance company or to theirs.

Negotiating 101

The test drive is over and it's obvious she wants your car. There is usually *a look in the eyes* that gives it away, and she has it. After some small talk she says, "I like the car. What's your best price?"

Now What?

Negotiating price is the least favorite part of buying or selling a car for most people. Yet if it works the way it should, you already have a relatively high Initial Asking Price. She makes a low offer, and you come to terms by meeting somewhere in the middle. Easy as pie.

Unfortunately, it usually doesn't work quite so easily.

In fact, why is it that what happens next is more like your first awkward date with Mary Beth in the 10th grade?

- You're scared to death to put your arm around her shoulder, and you're scared to death not to. Confusion reigns, and in the end you just want to get it over without embarrassing yourself too much.

Except this time it could cost you hundreds, if not thousands of dollars "just to get it over with."

Negotiating does not have to be confusing or difficult. And the answer doesn't lie in learning complex negotiating techniques. In the heat of battle, you'll forget those long before you can use them.

Learn from the pros: simple is better.

Street Smarts

What I'm about to tell you did not come from a text book. It's *street smarts*. It is the culmination of years of working with thousands of customers at the car dealership level. And working intimately with a variety of sales staff, sales managers, and "closers" who specialized in getting customers to say "yes" to deals, while paying the highest possible price to the dealership.

Pressure to Sell

People in car sales are "commissioned," meaning they sell cars or they don't get paid. And the more the dealership makes on a deal, the more commission the salesperson earns. This creates significant pressure to sell for the most they can get. If a salesperson wants to pay their rent, they need to sell lots and maximize profit on each deal.

You may be wondering if my years in the auto industry sent me over to the "dark side," turning me into a crass, manipulative car salesman, only interested in making money on each deal.

It is true that I had to survive in a "shark tank" by selling enough cars and earning enough commissions to pay my bills each month. My saving grace was to join the industry late in life. I wasn't about to sell my soul for a paycheck.

What I did was find a ***different path*** that allowed me to become one of the top salespeople at my dealership. All it took was a slight shift of perspective. Instead of focusing on the sale, I zeroed in on a different challenge: solving my customer's transportation problem!

And you thought I was going to say that the purpose of selling cars at a major dealership is to actually sell cars. It's true that the attitude of most dealers is to sell, sell, sell—at any cost—and they have the negative reputation to prove it.

You can learn from this. If you, as a private seller, only focus on how you can sell your car to *everyone* who contacts you, two things will happen:

- You will begin to embody the worst traits of used car salesmen by ignoring what the buyer wants. You will probably manipulate the situation (and the buyer) in order to sell her your car, whether she wants it or not, and whether it's appropriate for her or not.

- You will miss the best selling opportunity that is available to you: supporting your buyer's situation.

When you shift your perspective from **selling** to **problem solving**, it changes everything and allows you to get curious about your prospective buyer.

Find out what her actual needs are, how the vehicle will be used,
who will drive it, and her other concerns.

By aligning your approach to her actual situation, you become an ally instead of a combatant. You become a problem solver instead of a manipulator. More importantly, you'll stand a better chance of selling her your car!

The Price is Right

If there is one thing I learned by dealing with car buyers day in and day out over a period of years, it's that they inevitably have a price in mind that they want to pay.

The figure may be based on their own research, their budget, or what a friend suggests, but it's an actual price, *and it is their expectation.* However, it's usually not the first price they offer.

Your job is to find out what price she wants to pay. Most buyers want to keep this a secret of course, and will posture around it. Many will try to buy your car for thousands of dollars less than what it's worth. These initial attempts are pure blunder and posturing, and not real. Yet they sometimes work.

My negotiating advice addresses the majority of people that you will deal with:

The person who buys and sells a few cars in a lifetime
and who is out to get the best deal they can.

It is not for the five percent who car dealers call "grinders"—those savvy, ruthless, experienced negotiators. If you run across one of these, simply make your best case and walk away before they **grind you down** and get you to settle for far less than what you want.

My advice also does not cover the "lay downs"—those who simply lay down and accept whatever price you name. If you get one of these, acknowledge the blessings and quickly move on.

For the vast majority of buyers who aren't grinders or lay downs, here is a typical scenario:

- Everyone knows you have priced your car higher than market value to allow for negotiations. Your buyer does the same thing in reverse. She makes the offer knowing it's too low and is prepared to pay more.

Here's a specific example:

- I have estimated my 2006 Honda Civic to have a fair market value of $15,000. I set an Initial Selling Price of $15,900, allowing $900 for negotiating. I priced it high knowing I'll come down in price, but hope I'll get lucky and make a few hundred more than I expect. When I get an interested buyer, she offers $14,000. This tells me we will probably come to terms by meeting in the middle, somewhere around my estimated fair market value. I'm about as high as she is low. So far, so good.

Problems arise in the above scenario if the buyer offers you a significantly lower price than your initial selling price. If my buyer offers me $13,000 I know it will take work to ease them up to fair market value.

Use *The Force* . . .

In this case, The Force is the attitude of *problem solving* rather than *selling*, and asking questions rather than using tricks or manipulation. Try this:

> *Thanks for your offer. I'm hoping we can come to terms.*
> *But your offer is significantly lower than my asking price.*
>
> *How did you come to that specific figure?*
> *Is it based on your budget? Or on price research*
> *and what you feel comparable cars are selling for?*

They made an offer, but you haven't said anything about *your* price yet? You haven't justified it, defended it, or postured. At this point you are still **problem solving, not selling**.

You have also moved the conversation off **your** figure and onto **hers**. In fact, rather than justifying your price, she now has to defend her offer. Based on your research, she has no justification for such a low offer. Now it gets interesting.

Starting Point

Once she responds, you at least have a starting point
and an understanding of how she justifies her initial offer.

But you still haven't found her price yet, the one
that she actually expects to pay for your car.

It's time to build *your* case and explain why you set the price you did. There is nothing complicated about this next step. In fact, it comes down to simple common sense:

A Common Sense Response

I'm not a professional at this sort of thing.
All I want to do is sell my car for a fair price.

I went to KBB.com to find the current market value.
My Civic has low mileage and is in great condition.
So it's in high demand, which KBB takes into account.

Unfortunately, your price is well below what KBB says my car
should sell for. I'm flexible, but I have to ask you this question:
is there another price, one between your initial offer
and my asking price, that would work for you?

You justified your price, but didn't reduce it. And the ball is back in her court.

At this point, in my experience, the buyer knows their initial gambit isn't working and gives up attempting to steal the car for thousands less than what it's worth. Instead, they step up and name a price closer to what they are actually willing to pay.

Now you simply make the best argument you can. This should include:

- Lowering your price in small increments:

  Okay, I'm a little high. I guess if I have to, I can come down a few hundred dollars. Would that work for you?

- Passing the blame onto KBB as the third party expert who is responsible for setting your price:

  I let Kelly Blue Book set the price, and KBB says this car, with these miles, in this condition should sell for over $15,000 and that's what I've got it priced at.

- Keep reaffirming the features that drew her to your car in the first place:

  You said you're looking for a good commuter car. The Civic is a great commuter car. It gets incredible gas mileage—40 mpg on the highway.

  It has low miles so it will last longer than most other cars you'll find. You like the way it drives, and it's in great condition.

  You won't find many like this out there. Are you really willing to let this opportunity pass you by?

- Keep going back to her figures. Ask her to come up—even a little:

  Your price is still well below KBB. We're getting closer in price. You're at $14,500 and I'm at $15,700. I've already come down. Can't you help just little? You must have a few hundred more built into your offer?

- The final ploy on your part is to make an offer and stick to your position, only changing it to close the deal and shake hands:

  I'll tell you what. We are so close in price why don't we split the difference. I'll meet you in the middle at $15,100. I'm willing to settle, and you'll get a great commuter car.

  Do you really want to go through this whole process again with someone else, all for the sake of a few dollars? Why don't we wrap this up now?

When you ask a closing question—in this case, "Why don't we wrap this up now?"—don't say another word until the buyer speaks. There is an old adage in sales that after you ask her to buy the car for a specific price (a closing question), the first one who speaks loses.

What do I mean by "lose?" If she speaks first you've probably made the deal at the price you want. (She spoke first and you get the price *you* want.)

However, if you jump in to fill what can be an uncomfortable silence, you lose the momentum and will probably have to lower your price again to make the deal. (You spoke first and she gets the price *she* wants.)

When to Walk Away?

In my experience you may actually need to walk away in order to gain the respect of some buyers, before they will do business with you.

You reach a point where you say, "I'm sorry we can't come to terms, but I'm just not willing to sell my car for what you are offering. Let's agree that we can't agree on a price. Thanks anyway." And walk away.

If you get home without them stopping you, you can always call back and re-engage the negotiations by saying that you are willing to come down a few dollars, and will that work for them? If not, you haven't lost anything.

If they accept, you just sold your car. If they want to keep negotiating, well, you need to make a decision when enough is enough.

Let's Recap

Once you actually begin negotiating the price you should:

- Lower your price in small increments.
- Justify your price by quoting KBB as the authority who sets used car prices.
- Keep reaffirming the car's best features, based on her buying criteria.
- Keep asking her to raise her price.

There are a hundred other techniques you can use, but keep it simple and honest. So far you have done both:

- your ad was clear, transparent, and easy to understand.
- you answered her call promptly and didn't use gimmicks or tricks.
- you were honest and upfront when answering her questions and didn't try to cover up any defects.
- you were friendly and courteous when you showed the car, giving her as much time as she needed.
- you were flexible on the price, but she could tell you were also firm with your price because your car had value.

> *Just like you, a private buyer is more likely to*
> *make a purchase from someone they like and trust.*

You've earned their business. Congratulations!

12 Handling the Paperwork and Counting the Money

Be Confident - Be Safe

She wants to buy your car. You want to sell it to her. Together you have settled on the price. Now what? There are five remaining steps that still need attention:

1. The Bill of Sale
2. Clearing the outstanding loan
3. Getting paid
4. Transferring ownership
5. Handing over your keys

Each state has its own way of doing things. The final authority on how to sell a vehicle in your state is determined by the Department of Motor Vehicles (DMV).

I suggest you read this chapter, and then check with the local DMV to confirm the steps *you* need to take to complete the sale. The following should be considered only an outline, until you confirm with your DMV exactly what needs to be done and when.

1. The Bill of Sale

In most states a Bill of Sale does not actually transfer legal ownership of your car to the buyer. That's done through the DMV with the title transfer.

However, many states still require a Bill of Sale, and I recommend one too. It makes the transaction explicit—and when dealing with the legality of selling your car, agreeing on the basic information is a good first step. A Bill of Sale should include:

- the vehicle identification number (VIN)
- year, make, and model
- odometer reading (mileage)
- date of sale
- purchase price
- be sure to include the phrase *"sold as is,"* unless you have agreed to something else

- names and addresses of buyer and seller
- signatures of buyer and seller

To make sure you get it right, download a Bill of Sale online. For a small fee you can get a professional document that has been designed specifically for your state. You'll feel better and the buyer will have more confidence that you know what you're doing.

Get Your Forms Online

Simple is often better. You can now get a Bill of Sale online. This, and other useful information, is on the **Tools** page of my website at www.BayAreaCarGuy.com/tools.

2. Clearing the Outstanding Loan

When a bank, credit union, or financial institution lends you money to buy a car, they register a lien against the vehicle. This allows you to use the car, but not sell it. In most states, both your name and the bank's name are listed as owners on the title and on the vehicle registration.

*The vehicle registration stays with you;
the title stays with the DMV or the bank.*

You will only receive the physical title once the loan is paid off, except in the case of a few states where banks allow the buyer to hold the title while there is still a loan registered against the vehicle.

The easiest way to clear a lien is to pay it off at the bank prior to selling your car. As proof of payment, you receive a lien release document. You may have to file this with your local DMV in order to get the actual title. Some states allow banks to use a paperless title where they don't actually have physical possession of the document. This simplifies the process of getting the title in your hands. Check with your local DMV.

However, most of us don't have that kind of extra cash lying around. We need the proceeds of the sale of the vehicle in order to pay off the loan and clear the lien.

In *Chapter 2 – Getting Your Vehicle Ready*, I suggested that you contact your lender and ask for the "10-day payoff" figure. This is how much you will owe if you pay it off in the next ten days. I also suggested that you ask the bank to send you a fax stating that amount, so you can show it to your buyer.

This official copy of the payoff amount leaves no room for doubt on the amount needed to clear the lien. Even if you go beyond the ten days, it still provides an approximate figure for the buyer, and helps build confidence in you.

Upside Down?

If you owe more on the car than what you are selling it for, you have *negative equity*. Pros call it being *upside down*. This issue has become more common since the economy tanked and loan money dried up, causing used car prices to fluctuate.

If you are in a negative equity situation, you will need extra cash to make up the difference between the sale price and the amount you owe the bank. Can't get your hands on the extra cash? So sorry—you won't be selling your car today. No one wants to buy a car with a pre-existing lien because they will become financially responsible for the loan, facing the prospect of having the car repossessed if payments aren't made.

Anyway, banks generally won't approve a loan if the car isn't worth enough as collateral to secure the new loan.

Clearing the Lien

Once your loan is paid off, your bank will issue a lien release document, and the DMV will issue a new title free of all liens and encumbrances.

If you need money from the sale to pay off the loan, call the bank to confirm that staff will be available when you bring your buyer in. You will conduct the actual sale of the vehicle at the bank. Some states allow banks to do all the paperwork, including the DMV title transfer.

There are two possible scenarios:

- **Positive Equity** – The seller owes less than the selling price. The buyer pays the bank the outstanding amount of the loan, usually with a cashier's check or cash. (Personal checks delay the process till the check clears.)

  The balance—the difference between the loan payoff amount and the selling price—is paid by the buyer directly to you. A cashier's check or cash is normally used.

- **Negative Equity** – The seller owes more than the selling price. The buyer pays the bank the full selling price of the vehicle, usually with a cashier's check or cash. Because the seller is upside down on the loan, more is needed to clear the lien.

The seller pays the balance to the bank. Again, a cashier's check or cash is normally used. This way the buyer sees that the car is free of all liens and encumbrances.

An Out-Of-Town Bank?

What if the bank is out-of-town, out of state, or is a manufacturer's lending arm such as Ford Credit, GMAC, or Toyota Motor Credit? Are you out of luck? Not necessarily. The payoff can still be accomplished, though not as easily. In this case, I suggest you use Escrow.com to manage the transaction. There's more about escrow services in the next section.

If you want to handle the payoff yourself, and the bank is not local, here is how to go about it:

- **Confirm Payoff** – The buyer and seller use the *trust, but verify* principle. They complete a number of tasks together, each confirming that every step is taken care of.

  Together they call the bank to confirm the 10-day payoff figure, whom to make the payment payable to, where to send it, and get any other instructions from the bank.

  They also need to find out how to get the title once the bank receives payment. This varies, depending on the financial institution and the state.

- **Positive Equity** – The seller owes less than the selling price. The buyer provides a cashier's check payable to the bank in the amount of the 10-day payoff figure.

  Buyer and seller together put the cashier's check and instructions for the payoff (including information about the loan being paid off—name, account number, VIN) in an envelope, and mail it to the bank.

  The balance—the difference between the loan payoff figure and the selling price—is paid by the buyer directly to the seller with a cashier's check or cash.

- **Negative Equity** – The seller owes more than the selling price. The buyer provides a cashier's check payable to the bank for the selling price of the vehicle. Because the seller is upside down on the loan, more is needed to clear the lien.

  The seller also provides a cashier's check payable to the bank, for the balance needed to pay-off the loan. Together they put both cashier's checks and instructions (including information on the loan being paid off—name, account number, VIN) in an envelope and mail it to the bank.

In this way the buyer is assured the car will be free of all liens and encumbrances.

3. Getting Paid

There are many ways to complete payment on a used car transaction. Short of handling the transaction at a bank, no direct buyer-to-seller payment method is completely safe. Cashier checks can be forged, and carrying large amounts of cash runs its own risk.

I recommend that you use a state licensed, online escrow service. An escrow service acts as a middle-man, holding the money until the loan is paid off, then releasing funds in a safe manner.

These services are reasonably priced, especially when the fee is split between buyer and seller. They offer a level of safety that is priceless.

There are online escrow services that protect both buyer and seller, but you have to be on guard against fraudulent ones. Do not accept just any escrow service recommended by the buyer. When in doubt, use a reliable and licensed escrow service. Find out more on the **Tools** page of my website at www.BayAreaCar-Guy.com/tools.

If You Really Have to...

If using an escrow service is not an option, here are some suggestions:

- **Personal check** – I don't recommend that you take a personal check as payment for your vehicle. If the check bounces and is returned for insufficient funds, you are in real trouble.

  However, if you must accept a personal check, don't give physical possession of the car nor transfer the title to the buyer until the check has cleared the originating bank. This can take a week or more.

- **Cashier's check or money order** – It is unfortunate that what used to be a guaranteed form of payment can now be forged. For this reason I advise treating cashier's checks and money orders as personal checks.

Confirm its validity by taking it to a local bank prior to turning over title and physical possession. If the bank is out of town, wait until it clears the originating bank.

- **Accept only the exact amount of the price of the car** – There are active scams where the buyer sends you a cashier's check or money for more than the purchase price of the vehicle.

  They always have some bizarre rationale for doing it, like the last seller backed out of the deal, or they are out of the country and can't make changes to the form of payment. You are asked to wire the difference to the buyer, and in some cases to wire the entire amount.

  Problems arise when you discover that the original cashier's check or money order is bogus, and you are out the money you wired. Oops! There is no reason to accept a payment for more than the agreed price. Never wire a buyer money—for any reason.

- **Don't rush** – If the bank is closed when you complete the negotiations, wait until the bank guarantees funds before you turn over physical possession of your car and transfer legal title.

  Your physical possession of the car is the only way to control the transaction. If there is no easy way to complete the transaction safely, use an online escrow service (see the **Tools** page of my website at www.BayAreaCarGuy.com/tools).

4. Transfer Ownership

Regulations vary by state, so check with your local DMV.

- **Bill of Sale** – Not all states require a Bill of Sale, but I recommend that you complete one anyway. It clarifies all basic terms of the sale in a useful way. Details above in *1. Bill of Sale*.

- **Title** – If you don't have the title but own your vehicle outright (no loan), contact your local DMV for a replacement well before you plan to sell your vehicle.

  If you have a loan on your car, contact your lender or refer back to *2. Clearing the Outstanding Loan*.

- **Future liability** – Once you transfer legal ownership to the buyer, you want to avoid future liability of having your name attached to the vehicle. For example, once you sell the car you don't want to be responsible for:

– the new buyer's unpaid parking tickets

– future state registration fees

– the vehicle's involvement in an accident

Most states require you to complete something similar to California's *Notice of Transfer & Release of Liability* form immediately following the sale. Ask for the correct form at the DMV in your state. Here are a few more considerations:

- **License plates** – Do you leave the license plates on the car or return them to the DMV? This varies by state, so check with your local DMV prior to transferring ownership.

- **Smog Inspection** – Some vehicles require a smog inspection certificate prior to the new owner registering it in their name. Check with your local DMV to see who is responsible for providing (and paying for) the certificate.

- **Copies** – Make sure that you get copies of all paperwork.

5. Handing Keys (And the Vehicle) Over to the New Buyer

Once all payment and transfer issues have been resolved, you can give physical possession of the car to the buyer. Leave whatever might be useful for the new owner, such as the owner's manuals, and take everything of yours.

Carefully check:

- under the seats and floor mats.

- in the glove box, cubby holes front and rear, and the trunk, including in the spare tire wheel well.

- look for CDs or DVDs in the player(s), and in CD holders attached to the driver or passenger visors or in the center console.

- spare change in the coin holder.

- is anything hanging from the rear view mirror?

- do you have personalized license plates, license plate frames, special floor mats, or other equipment not included in the sale that you want to take with you?

Perform a final walk-around to make sure you have all your personal possessions. Most buyers also want to do their own walk-around and inspect the vehicle to confirm its condition.

Once you physically hand the keys over to the buyer and have filed your release of liability form with the DMV, cancel your vehicle insurance.

Shipping a Vehicle

Some out-of-town buyers want the vehicle shipped instead of picking it up in person. Shippers generally use large hauling trucks. Prices start in the hundreds of dollars, but vary depending on the length of the haul and the weight of the car.

By this stage of the selling process, shipping costs should already have been negotiated. For more information on dependable auto shippers see the **Tools** page of my website at www.BayAreaCarGuy.com/tools.

Get Online Resources for Selling Your Car
at www.BayAreaCarGuy.com

BayAreaCarGuy.com is a companion website to *HELP! I Gotta Sell My Car NOW!* Discover these resources:

- **Photo page** – Photo layouts for all major websites. Discover which photos to use and the order to upload when posting your ad online.

- **Video page** – Examples of how to record your video walk-around. This is the secret weapon that's easy to use. Become a YouTube star.

- **Tools page** – Tons of other FREE tools to help you sell your car.

- **Need Help? page** – Two services offered depending on your level of expertise:

  - **The Quick Consult** – One for private sellers and one for car dealers. I'm available to answer questions, including—for private sellers—how to price your car.

  - **Write My Ad** – The name says it all. Private sellers get an effective ad and a pricing strategy. I also check in weekly until your car sells. It's like having your personal Automotive Consultant on call.

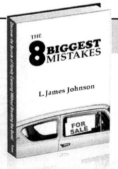

Also written by L. James Johnson

The 8 Biggest Mistakes Used Car Buyers Make And How to Avoid Them!

DOWNLOAD
FREE PDF

 (3.15mb)

Download your FREE
18-page PDF online at
www.BayAreaCarGuy.com

Here is what auto professionals have to say about *The 8 Biggest Mistakes*:

"Don't buy a used car without reading The 8 Biggest Mistakes."
Stephanie Peters
Internet Sales Manager & 15-year car industry veteran

"A quick read. 18 pages that can save you thousands of dollars."
Rob Wilbur
Used Car Manager & 25-year car industry veteran

CPSIA information can be obtained
at www.ICGtesting.com
Printed in the USA
BVHW051123060321
601818BV00011BA/1490